Tears

by

David McCormac

About the Author

David McCormac was born in a small town called Iserlohn in the western part of Germany.

He was the second son to Geoffrey and Iris McCormac. Geoffrey an officer in the British Army and Iris a wonderful and loving mother.

After six months of living in Germany, David moved back to England and to his mother's home town of Nottingham.

After being state educated, David went to a university in London, where he read History. After three years David did a P.G.C.E in Northampton and a year later moved back to Nottingham where he has been teaching for the last twenty-five years.

Contents

Saint Mo

Characters

Mary

She is of medium height and has a slim figure. She has a quiet nature and shows much pain through her eyes due to the sexual abuse she has suffered through parts of her life. She is seventeen and she is the oldest child of Vile Vee.

Billy

He is a nine year-old boy and of average height for his age. He has black hair and blue eyes. He also gets himself in a lot of trouble, whether this is at school or with the police. He is the oldest boy of Vile Vee.

Tommy/Jenny

The two youngest children of Vile Vee. Tommy is three and Jenny is two.

The remaining characters are Mo, Harold, Brenda, Dick, Vile Vee and Do One Ron.

Setting

Mo's home.

Saint Mo

Dick and Brenda are knocking on Mo's door. Mo opens the door.

Mo

Good morning you two, come on, get yourself in *(they all go into the living room where Brenda and Dick sit down on the sofa)* Is it tea or coffee?

Brenda

Tea would be nice.

Dick

Tea for me too please.

Mo goes into the kitchen to make the tea. Leaving Brenda and Dick on the sofa. They both look at each other with worried looks. Mo comes back into the living room with the tea and biscuits. She passes the tea first to Brenda, then to Dick.

Mo

Help yourself to sugar and biscuits.

Brenda

Thank you Mo.

Mo

(Sitting down) Now how are you both and how are your wedding preparations going?

Brenda

We are fine, and as for the wedding, we have just about sorted it, although Dick is having problems finding a best man, that isn't an alcoholic or at her majesty's pleasure. We did think about asking Harold as he has been a good friend to us both over the years, especially Dick when he was getting drunk night after night. Harold was always there to pick him up and to make sure he had a bed for the night, either at his place or a hospital bed. In fact the hospital staff always said 'here comes piss head Dick' and in the morning when Dick's head was banging, the staff would get round his bed and say 'Dick head, Dick head' and they would all point to Dick. Mind you, things have changed.

Dick
For the better. *(He goes to hold Brenda's hand)*

Mo
How are you getting on with starting a family?

Brenda
(In a low voice) Do you know Mo, we have tried every position at every hour of the day, but nothing is working. In fact one book I read said you will have a better chance of getting pregnant if you keep your legs up during sex. Well Mo, I was walking like a bloody robot the next day. It's not every day you have to stand up to have a wee. *(They all laugh)* Sadly we just have to admit that my clock has stopped ticking and Dick's sperm has died in many a beer bottle.

Mo
But if you had the chance to have children how would you feel?

Brenda
Mo, If I had the chance, I would crawl on my hands and knees to find them, but my name is not Mary and no-one is going to bless me.

Mo
Did you hear about Vee on the market?

Brenda

Yes, Zit Face Zina was talking about it in the post office. She said that Vee hadn't got long and that her four children would have to go into care. It's such a shame, especially as her two youngest are under five.

Mo

You're right Brenda, her two youngest are under five, and Brenda, they are not going into care. *(As Mo says this Dick could be seen with tears running down his cheeks with his hands over his face)*

Brenda

Dick, what's happened? Why are you crying? Mo, what's going on?

Mo

They are not going into care because I hope you will adopt them.

Brenda

(Tears start to run down Brenda's face) Mo, please don't joke about this.

Mo

Believe me love, I'm not joking. *(Brenda collapses on the floor in tears. Dick gets down and holds her)*

Brenda

(Facing Mo) Thank you so much Mo, you are a saint.

Mo

And, so are you Brenda. Now get yourself up and dry those tears. *(she does this)* I want you to be here for nine o'clock Saturday morning, so you can pick up the children and spend the day with them. If it goes well then you will sign the papers that I have drawn up and in a weeks time the children will be yours.

Brenda

I'll be here on the dot. *(They all stand up and walk towards the door)* Thank you so much Mo. *(She embraces Mo and kisses her on her cheek)*

As they walk down the path, Brenda turns to face Mo and blows her a kiss. An hour later Harold knocks on the door. Mo opens it.

Mo

Hello Harold, come in love.

Harold

Thanks love.

Mo

Sit yourself down, any coffee?

Harold

Not for me love, my water works are playing up something shocking.

Mo

Is it?

Harold

It is love. I've been to the toilet so many times, I've made a bed up in the bath. Well it saves time, and as for the aroma, it's as though I've been eating sugar puffs twenty four seven. Now before I start running to your bathroom, what's up then love?

Mo

Well I'm sure you have heard about Vee from the market stall?

Harold

I have Mo, terrible. I know she was no saint, in fact you could say she was more linked to the devil. The amount of men she sucked the life out of, she should have been the bride of Dracula, sucking money up instead of blood. But for all that poor woman's sins, you wouldn't wish that on your worst enemy. The suffering she is going through must be terrible. I heard she only has a few weeks left.

Mo

She will be lucky to survive to the end of the month. You know she has four children?

Harold

I thought it would have been more.

Mo

Well her oldest daughter, who has just turned seventeen, needs a.. *(Harold interrupts)*

Harold

Yes.

Mo

Yes what?

Harold

The answer is yes Mo.

Mo

You don't know what I'm going to ask you.

Harold

You are going to ask if I will adopt her and the answer is yes.

Mo

I was, but there are issues.

Harold

Let me guess. For most of her childhood she has seen and felt rape and abuse and knowing her mother and the different men she has invited back after getting a free night out. I expect her daughter had many men come to her room in the middle of the night and force her to perform many sexual acts. To have a full grown man force his penis inside of you when you are only ten and when it came out, to then force your mouth around it and be told I've forgot the strawberries, but here comes the cream is agonizing and when he has finished, to walk out of the door saying 'this will be our secret and I'll bring you some sweeties next time.' You feel so used and alone as the blood trickles from your bottom. What is her name?

Mo

Mary.

Harold

Blessed will be her life from now on.

Mo

(With tears running down her face) Will you pick her up at nine on Saturday, so you can spend the day with her?

Harold

I will be here at nine.

They both get up and hug. As Harold walks down the garden path, he turns with tears in his eyes and waves.

Mo

(To herself) Two down, one to go.

Half an hour later Bucket Bill knocks on Mo's door. Mo opens the door.

Mo

Well it's so nice of you to pop round Bill, and on time. Have the pubs thrown you out or is it the women in your life, all have headaches?

Bill

Hello Mo, it's lovely to see you too.

Mo

I bet it is. Get yourself into the living room. I would tell you to take your shoes off, but they look like the cleanest things on you.

Bill

So what have you got in mind? I thought it was Janice who wanted it.

Mo

Bill you are a dirty, filthy pig who I wouldn't touch if I was blind drunk. However, some fool of a woman allowed you to get on top of her, resulting in a child, a child who is nine years old and is soon to lose his mother.

Bill

If you are talking about that money grabbing slut Vee, then she deserves what's coming to her.

Mo

That as maybe in your eyes, but a nine year old boy doesn't deserve the next seven years in a care home with no love or hope of happiness.

Bill

So what do you want me to do about it?

Mo

I'll tell you what you are going to do Bill and that is for the next seven years you will have your son stay with you every Friday and Saturday night.

Bill
Don't be bloody stupid woman.

Mo
You will pick him up from here at four thirty in the afternoon and you will bring him back at six o' clock Sunday evening.

Bill
I work on the stall Saturday's. Then I'm out with the lads Saturday night, so I can't help you.

Mo
Is that right Bill?

Bill
I'm afraid it is. He will be better off in care.

Mo
(On hearing this Mo's anger raises) Now you listen to me you worthless piece of crap. If you don't look after your own son at the weekends, I will make your life hell. Not only will I knock on every door in this village and tell them what a low life you are, but I will also tell every husband of the wives you have climbed on top of. You will be a dead man walking.

Bill
You bitch.

Mo
And don't you forget it. I suggest he helps you on the stall and Bill, you will pay him the correct money. I'll see you two weeks on Friday. It will take you two weeks to clean that hovel you call a home and to get his bedroom ready. I'll see you out. *(As Bill walks down the path, Mo shouts out)* Two weeks Friday! *(Bill sticks two fingers up and keeps on walking)*

Five minutes later there is a knock on the door. Coming to the door Mo can be heard talking loudly.

Mo

I've told you Bill, be at mine for four thirty, two weeks on Friday, or say hello to hell. *(She opens the door and sees Ron standing there. Blushing bright red, she smiles)*

Ron

Well I don't know about hell, but I'm in heaven looking at you.

Mo

Hello Ron, do you want a coffee?

Ron

(Walking into the house) I would love one in about two hours time.

Mo

Why in two hours?

Ron

Because I'm going to be very busy.

Mo

What with?

Ron

You. *(He picks her up and carries her upstairs)*

End of a life

Characters

Mo, Brenda and Dick, Harold, Vee, Mary, Billy, Tommy and Jenny.

Setting

Mo's home and Vee's home.

End of a Life

Mo is standing at the open door when Brenda and Dick, with the two children, come up the garden path

Mo

Well here they come, "The Adam's Family". *(They all laugh)* The children run after the cat into the house.

Brenda

(Hugging Mo) what a day.

Dick

(With tears in his eyes, he hugs a surprised Mo) Thank you.

Mo

(Shouting) Billy get your brother and sister a drink, then go and play in the garden. Come and have a sit down you two. How have you got on today?

Brenda

Oh Mo, you wouldn't believe the stuff that comes out of their mouths and talk about bulging pockets after every shop we went into. They had taken everything they could get their hands on. In fact we spent half the day taking back everything they had nicked. When we went into the supermarket, little Tommy went up to the security guard and said 'hey twat face, who are you looking at?' As I rushed over, do you know what the guard said to me?

Mo

What?

Brenda

He said 'would you kindly keep your son under control.' Mo, he said my son. I was in heaven. I didn't even check his pockets when we left. Mind you, the best bit was when we went to the cinema to see 'The Little Mermaid.' Half way through it, Tommy stood up and shouted, 'she's too young for me, I'll have the mother.' I didn't know where to put my face. Then five minutes later little Jenny starts to cry, saying 'all this water has made my front bottom drip.' The seat was soaking wet. I thought it would be best to leave before the end.

Mo

So do I detect a few doubts creeping in?

Brenda

There are no doubts in our minds, give us the papers now and we will sign.

Mo

You will have to wait until next Saturday, Vee wants you to collect them from her place.

Brenda

Of course she wants to have them for one last week. Is she coming to the end?

Mo

They are saying two weeks at the most.

There is a knock at the door. Mo opens the door.

Harold

Hiya Mo. Here we are safe and sound.

Mo

Come in you two. Mary, your brothers and sister are in the garden. *(She walks out into the garden. Harold goes into the living room and hugs both Brenda and Dick)* Sit yourself down love. Now, how has it gone?

Harold

Mo, we have had a lovely day. We first went round the shops. I got her a couple of outfits, well at seventeen you can't be wearing your mother's cast offs. Then we went to that new Chinese restaurant up saucy road. Talking about saucy, the waiters were to die for. These black trousers they wear, left very little to the imagination. I dropped my knife twice on the floor, hoping a waiter would split his trousers when he picked it up. Mind you, he did give me extra crispy duck.

Mo

He must of thought one old bird to another. *(They all laugh)*

Harold

You cheeky mare.

Mo

How did Mary like it?

Harold

Well she didn't say a lot. But when you have never been bought new clothes or eaten in a restaurant before, I think her new surroundings left her speechless. But her smile did mask the sadness in her eyes for a time.

Brenda

What about your Herbert?

Harold

What about him love?

Brenda

He will be living under the same roof?

Harold

Now you're asking.

Mo

What's happened?

Harold

Well, all I heard from him this morning was, 'do you think you're doing the right thing? How much money will it cost you? And you have to think about your age.' I turned round to him and said 'if it had been a seventeen year old boy, you would be glad to look after him, with your wandering hands. But as it is a seventeen year old girl, you're not interested.' So I said 'if you don't like it, there's the door.' I've not seen him since.

Mo

But you can't let this come between you Harold.

Harold

Mo love, the only thing that has been between us for years is a relationship that was rotten. You and Mary have given me hope for a new life.

Mo

Can you be around Vee's place next Saturday to collect the papers?

Harold

I'll be there. *(There is a knock on the door)*

Mo

That will be Ron to take the children back.

Harold

Is that Do One Ron?

Mo

My friend Ron.

Harold

I heard he was a friend with benefits.

Mo

I don't know what you mean.

Harold

Benefits that extend to the bedroom. I heard you had left your bedroom window open and a group of locals were monitoring the noise pollution coming from your bedroom. They said Heathrow was quieter *(red faced Mo goes to let Ron in)*

Ron

Hello beautiful, are the children ready? *(He walks through to the living room)* Hello Harold, hello Brenda and Dick.

Harold

Hello Ron, or is that rodgering Ron? It's so nice to see you looking after Mo's needs.

Harold/Brenda

(Singing) 'keep smiling, keep shining, knowing you can always count on me for sure, that's what friends are for. *(They all sing the last line. They all laugh)*

Mo

You lot get worse. I'll fetch the children. *(Two minutes later the children come into the living room)* It's time to go. You only have a week left at your mother's and I want you to promise me you will be as good as gold. You know your mother will be in heaven soon.

Tommy

She will be a star shining down on us. *(There is a minute's silence.)*

Harold

What a nice friend to have.

Brenda

A very nice friend.

Dick

A very, very nice friend.

Mo

Piss off the lot of you. *(They all laugh)*

A week later they all arrive at Vee's house.

Mo

(As they assemble at the door) This is not going to be easy.

Brenda

But for the children, it will be worth it. *(Mo knocks at the door. Mary opens it)*

Mo

Hello Mary, can we come in?

Mary

Yes, mother is in the sitting room, she wants Brenda and Dick to go in first. *(Brenda and Dick follow Mary to the sitting room. Mary shuts the door and goes into the kitchen)*

Vee

Please sit down. *(They both sit down on a well worn sofa, that is in a sparsely decorated room. They both look towards Vee, who's appearance is disturbing. She has a pale, withdrawn face that is resting on a painfully thin body. Her hair is a mixture of white and grey with her eyes red and bulging)* I want to thank you so much for agreeing to take Tommy and Jenny. They are wonderful children and I know they will be very happy with you both. Love them please, like I have. I might not have been able to give them much in the way of material things, but they never went without a mother's love. *(Brenda has tears running down her cheeks)*

Brenda

Vee, we will give them all our love and thank you for trusting us with your children.

Vee

(She passes them an envelope) Everything is signed. Good luck to you both. *(The door opens and Mo can be seen holding Tommy and Jenny's hand)* Come and give me a hug my darlings. *(The children walk over to their mother and she hugs them both)* Now I want you to promise me that you will be as good as gold for your new Mummy and Daddy. And every night I want you to look up into the sky and I will be one of those stars shining down on you. *(A tear trickles down her cheek)* Goodbye my darlings. *(Brenda and Dick take the children by their hands and lead them to the door. As they get to the door Tommy turns around to face his mother)*

Tommy

Bye bye Mummy *(Vee blows him a kiss which he catches and puts to his heart. They go out and shut the door. After both hugging Mo with tears streaming down their faces, they open the front door and take their new son and daughter with them)*

Harold

It looks like it's my turn now.

Mo

Are you sure?

Harold

I've never been more sure about anything in my life. *(Harold stands up and opens the door)*

Vee

Come in Harold. *(He closes the door and sits down)* I must first thank you from the bottom of my heart for what you have done for me and for Mary. I will agree that she has not had the best of times, especially when we didn't know where the next meal was coming from. At times we sat in the cold because we didn't have any money for the meter, but I will say one thing in my defence, none of my children went without love and I would like to think I was always there for them. Harold, can I ask you one favour?

Harold

Of course.

Vee

If she gets her qualifications will you let her go to university?

Harold

Vee, you can rest assure she will get her qualifications and she will go to university. I know she will do us both proud. *(She gives him an envelope with the signed papers in it)*

Vee

Thank you Harold. God be with you both. *(The door opens and Mary comes into the room)* 'Mary, come and give me a hug. I'm going to miss you so much. You be a wonderful daughter to Harold. Work hard and I will be with you in spirit in every part of your life. Goodbye my darling. *(With tears streaming down Mary's face she gets up and goes to the door with Harold. As she gets to the door she turns round)*

Mary

Goodbye Mum. *(They both go out the door)*

Mo

Are you alright my darling?

Harold

(He hugs Mo with tears in his eyes) Do you know Mo, I wanted to be a father all my life and just like the mother of John the Baptist we were blessed in our later years of life. Thank you Mo for being such a wonderful, wonderful human being. *(He takes Mary's hand and they walk out of the door)*

With only Mo and Billy left, Mo goes into the sitting room and sits down on the sofa.

Vee

Well Mo, you have done what you said you would. I will be honest, I did not think you would achieve it, but I was so wrong. You are a remarkable woman Mo and you so deserve the name Saint Mo. From my heart I thank you so much. *(She holds Mo's hand)* Now I know and you know that our Billy is the most challenging, but I know you won't take any crap. I hear you are seeing someone, so you won't be on your own.

Mo

I see good news travels fast.

Vee

I think it was you leaving your bedroom window open that gave the game away. Is he that good?

Mo

Let's just say the earth moved more than once.

Vee

Well good luck to you, we all deserve a bit of happiness. Please love Billy like I have.

Mo

You don't need to worry, I will look after all his needs.

Vee

Mo, I have put your name on my bank account and here are four envelopes with a cheque in each one for ten thousand pounds.

Mo

Bloody hell Vee.

Vee

Now you know why so many said I was a grabbing bitch. I didn't lay on my back for the pleasure, it was for my children's future. You will know when the right time is Mo, to give them their cheques. *(As she finishes talking the door opens and Billy, with tears in his eyes, rushes into his mother's open arms)* I'm going to miss you so much, but I want you to promise me you will be as good as gold for Auntie Mo and work hard at school and go to bed when you are told.

Billy

I will Mummy.

Vee

And don't forget I will always be with you. Look up each night and I will be that shining star looking down to see that you are being a good boy who is very happy.

Billy

I will be a good boy Mummy.

Vee

Goodbye Mo. God be with you both. *(Mo gets up and leads Billy to the door. As she opens the door, Billy turns to face his mother)*

Billy

Goodbye Mummy.

Vee

Goodbye my darling. *(She blows him a kiss)*

When Mo and Billy leave the house, Vee is left all alone. She gets up and slowly walks to the stairs. In great pain and exhaustion, she climbs the stairs to reach each of her children's bedroom.

She stands at Mary's bedroom door and remembers back to when Mary was sitting down, trying makeup on. She remembers going over to her and putting her arms around her and when their faces are cheek to cheek she says 'never cover up your beauty.' They both smile.

She then struggles to Billy's room and remembers him fast asleep. She remembers going over to him and kissing him on the cheek and saying 'I don't know what life has in store for you, but I love you so much!'

Finally she goes to Tommy's and Jenny's room. She remembers going into their bedroom and saying 'are you two not asleep yet?' and Jenny asking if she could read them a story. Just a quick one. 'What would you like me to read?' 'Sleeping Beauty please.' When Vee gets to the end of the story she tells Jenny she is a beautiful princess and that a prince will come and kiss her. As Vee is looking at the bed she remembers telling Tommy not to worry as he is the prince in Cinderella. She can see herself putting them back into their beds and telling them how much she loves them.

As she makes her way back down the stairs, with tears streaming down her face, she stops at her window and can see her reflection looking back at her. Seeing how the cancer has ravaged her face she can be heard saying "goodbye" to her children, through her cancer ridden mouth. Two minutes later she collapses onto the floor and all is quiet.

In church Mo is talking from the pulpit.

Mo

I would first like to thank all of you for coming and I want to give a special thank you to the market traders for closing their stalls, so they could give their respects to a woman who has been a part of their lives for so many years. I think we would all agree that Vee was never the easiest of people to get on with and if you were to have the misfortune to ever cross her you knew you were in for a bumpy ride. Yes when it came to money, Vee put the d into dishonest. But when it came to her children no one could say that she didn't try her best. Yes she did make mistakes, whether it was a week on the gin or a robbing spree at the shops. But I define anyone who says that she did not love her children, only wanting the best for them. Believe me, when you have to say goodbye to your children for the last time and then have to watch as new parents lead them away, is something no mother should ever have to do. But I swear to you now Vee, your children will be given the same love and devotion as you gave, and God willing they will flourish throughout all of their life.

(As Mo descends the steps of the pulpit everyone in the church stands up. Mo is seen walking up the aisle holding Billy's hand)

Blow and Go

Characters

Mo, Phoebe, Janice, Vera Virus, Frigging Freda, The Fella Bella and Harold.

Setting

The hairdressers, Blow and Go.

Blow and Go

Mo walks into the hairdressers, she is confronted by customers, making moaning sounds that would happen during sex.

Vera Virus

Here she is, mother with child.

Mo

Piss off you lot, I don't know what you are suggesting with these moaning noises.

Vera Virus

I bet you don't, you tart. Taking advantage of a younger man. I heard you had a letter from the environmental health department complaining about the noise pollution coming from your bedroom. *(They all laugh)*

Mo

I can assure you no one has said a word about me or my shy friend. *(They all laugh)* In fact I tell a lie. That Mrs Clark from two doors down, was banging on my door at ten o' clock the other night. I opened the door and off she starts. She said I've just found out my Georgina is pregnant and I'm sure it was your cat that has taken advantage of her virginity. Is that right, I said. Then she said, I don't think so, I know so, like mother, like son. If his mother can make loud moaning noises, what chance has her cat got. You need to set your cat a better example.

Janice

She didn't.

Mo

She did and wait for it, she then said I should go back to my

Peter Rabbit, that way we can all get some sleep.

Janice
Mo, that's shocking.

Mo
And there's more. She said I think it would only be fair if I paid her some compensation for what my cat had done to her innocent Georgina. By this time I had had enough. I said, you think so do you? Well, firstly your Georgina should have put her paw over her tuppence, unlike her mother did. And also I heard every time you were at a bus stop, you had to shut your legs incase the bus took a wrong turn and ended up inside you. How dare you, she said. Then I said, seeing as my Tabatha is a female cat, I don't think there is much chance of her being the father, now piss off.

Phoebe
I'm surprised you didn't slap her.

Mo
Let's just say if I didn't have me trousers on, with the pockets in, I might have forgotten she was ninety two.

The Fella Bella comes out of the back of the shop

The Fella Bella
Is that Saint Mo? I've just got to give you a hug, you are amazing. *(He hugs Mo)*

Mo
Bella, you are a star. Now what's this I've been hearing about your last date?

The Fella Bella
Mo, never again.

Mo
What happened?

The Fella Bella
Well, after putting my smalls in the washer.

Phoebe
That reminds me, I must get some washing powder.

The Fella Bella
What sort do you have?

Phoebe
Well I used to buy that one that smells like lavender.

The Fella Bella
No 'Fresh Summer?'

Phoebe
That's the one, we had it in the shop. On the box it said 'smell like nature on a summer's day.' Well the smell attracted nature alright.

Janice
Did it?

Phoebe
It definitely did. I was walking in the park and all of a sudden a group of bees started buzzing around my bits.

Vera Virus
No?

Phoebe
They could smell my lavender knickers.

Vera Virus

It makes a change that you had any on.

Everyone

(They all look at Vera Virus) Bitch.

Phoebe

So there I am trying to bat them away, when an old bloke sitting on a bench said 'are you alright love? It's nice to see you can still attract something.'

Janice

Nasty man.

Phoebe

Next minute I started running towards the gate. When I got to the gate there were two old dears sitting on a bench. I heard one of them say to her friend 'she must be on that new spice stuff, they call Manba.' As soon as I got home, I got them straight off. Never again.

Janice

You didn't throw them away?

Phoebe

No, I put them in a bag and took them round to Pervy Pete on front street.

Janice

You didn't?

Phoebe

I did. Well it was his birthday. At his age, there's not much chance of him nicking my underwear. He can't reach the washing lines anymore. He gave me a nice piece of fish to say thanks.

Mo

Have you no shame woman?

Phoebe

You have got to do your bit for the community.

The Fella Bella

It might have been bees for you, but it was nuts with me.

Vera Virus

Who's nuts?

The Fella Bella

My nuts.

Vera Virus

What was up with them?

The Fella Bella

Couldn't stop scratching them.

Vera Virus

No?

The Fella Bella

Yes. Well, what it was, I was going clubbing one Saturday night, so I thought it would be best to wash my underwear as you do. Anyway, I got to the club in my skin tight dress when a very handsome guy came over to see if he could buy me a drink. Well what is a girl supposed to do. So there we are talking away, when he asked me if I wanted to dance. Well it would have been rude not to say yes. So we are dancing away, when all of a sudden my lower bits started itching, well in that dress there was know where to hide and once I started to scratch I couldn't stop. The bloke's face was a picture. Do you know what he said?

Mo

What?

The Fella Bella
He said, I don't know why you had a champagne cocktail, rough blokes like you drink pints. He stormed off.

Mo
He never.

The Fella Bella
He did. Even in the taxi going home, the taxi driver said 'how much you selling your crabs for?'

Mo
That's not nice.

The Fella Bella
I'm telling you, as soon as I got in I bathed them for two hours, they were red raw.

Janice
I've never ever seen a red nut.

Mo
Or any other colour.

Janice
How rude. *(Laughing)*

Mo
Anyway you were saying about your last date.

The Fella Bella
So I was. So after putting the washer on I thought I've got half an hour free, so I went online and found this dating app 'Trans with and without bits.' I was only on it two minutes when this guy called Will, who was in his mid fifties, messaged me. He started with the usual crap, 'Hi beautiful, now I know where that missing star has

gone.' Then he said 'are you still modelling?'

Mo

Did you have a bucket handy?

The Fella Bella

Well after several yawns, I was just about to block him when he said 'do you fancy going for an Italian tomorrow night?' Well I was going to say no, but then I thought why not, if he's not much to look at, the waiters will be. Anyway I got there to find that he was waiting for me with a glass of champagne.

Mo

You don't get that every day.

The Fella Bella

Mo, I don't get that any day. So anyway, the meal came, he poured me some more champagne and just as I was about to take my first mouth full he started. He said, 'let me tell you something about myself. I live on my own now, but I did have a wife for twenty years.' 'Oh' I said. 'Did you? Why are you not together then?' He said she kept making mistakes with the house work. 'Like what?' I said. He replied, 'Well after she had washed and ironed my clothes, she not only didn't fold them properly, but would put them away in the wrong drawers. This made me very unhappy' he said. 'She never used the right scissors to cut the grass.' I said, 'that must have been terrible for you?' He said it was and it kept him awake many a night.

Mo

Did you run?

The Fella Bella

I would have done, but I hadn't had my desert. So then he said 'I've always wanted children and was looking for a woman to breed with.'

Janice

He didn't?

The Fella Bella

He did, what's more he said, 'with your youth and strength, I'm sure we will be able to have at least four.'

Mo

Bella, No!

The Fella Bella

Oh yes, finishing my desert, I said to him, 'you know the dating app we first met on, Trans with and without bits?!' He nodded. 'Well my bits down below allow me to stand up when I go for a wee.' Well Mo, his face dropped like Tina Tart's knickers on a Saturday night.

Vera Virus

That quick?

The Fella Bella

Next minute he said 'I must just pop to the toilet.' That was the last time I saw him. After sitting there for ten minutes, the waiter came over with the bill. I said 'I'm very sorry but I've not got any money on me, my friend was supposed to pay.' Next minute the manager came over and said 'I hear you can't pay your bill?' I said 'I can't.' 'Well in that case' he said 'if you don't want me to phone the police, you better come with me.' I had to wash up for three hours.

Janice

That's shocking.

The Fella Bella

What's more, it ruined my nails.

Vera Virus

That must have been the worst thing ever?

The Fella Bella
It was.

Frigging Freda
Hello everyone. I must give you a hug Mo *(they hug)* it's not every day you get to hug a living saint.

Mo
Give over with you.

Frigging Freda
What's this i've heard about Fat Stella?

Vera Virus
Have you not heard?

Mo
No, what's happened?

Vera Virus
Well I wasn't going to say anything but now you have asked. She is in a psychiatric unit because she thinks she is anorexic.

Frigging Freda
She doesn't?

Vera Virus
She does.

Frigging Freda
I heard she is in a bad way. What brought this on?

Vera Virus
Well, she went to the chippy last Friday night and while she was standing in the queue there was a power cut and everything switched off. Next minute the owner started to shout out 'we have

only got salad tonight.' Well with the alcohol sozzling her brain and her eating a lettuce leaf, she naturally thinks she is anorexic. I've heard while she has been in rehab she has lost over two stone.

Phoebe
There's always a silver lining.

Frigging Freda
Your hair is looking wonderful Mo. I hear you are off to some posh wedding.

Vera Virus
Are you Mo? If I had known that I would have spent a bit more time on it.

Frigging Freda
It's so nice to see you give your customers their money's worth. I hear you are going with the Duke.

Mo
Well we have been friends for many years.

Frigging Freda
Friends with benefits.

Mo
I don't know what you mean.

Frigging Freda
I nearly forgot, I saw Harold in the post office. He said he's popping over to make an announcement. Here he comes now.

Harold enters the hairdressers.

Harold
Hiya everyone.

All

Hiya Harold.

Mo

Are you alright love?

Harold

I'm good, apart from that zit face. Do you know what she said to me?

All

What?

Harold

She said, 'do you want these letters going first or second class?' I said first of course. Then the bitch said 'Harold, love, some people should know their place.

Mo

She didn't?

Harold

I said 'the only place you belong is a dermatologist's waiting room so you can have your puss filled spots sorted.' She stuck two fingers up at me when I was leaving.

Mo

She becomes more bitter everyday that one. Anyway Harold, what is it you want to announce?

Harold

Well I'm in a bit of a pickle. I've had the BBC on the phone. They want our quiz team to play against the 'Egg Yolks.'

Mo

That's great news.

Harold

Well it would have been if I had a quiz team to send.

Mo

Where are they all?

Harold

It's the same day we play the 'Interlocking Dogs' in the regional finale.

Mo

Why did they give themselves that name?

Harold

Well they wanted a name which showed them as a force that was locked together to defeat their rivals. Mind you, looking at the women in their team, you wouldn't want to be locked in with those couple of bitches. *(They all laugh)* So I'm happy to go to the BBC as I'm only the first reserve, but I need four other players.

Phoebe

Harold, don't worry love, we will get you four players. We will sort it.

Harold

Phoebe you are a star. I'll leave it with you. I must get home. Mary's feeling the stress with only three months to go before her exams. See you all later.

All

Bye Harold.

Mo

Bloody hell, look at the time, I've got to go and pick up Billy.

The Fella Bella

How's he doing love?

Mo

Getting better. A few weeks ago it seemed I was up at the school everyday. He was either fighting or telling the teacher to piss off, but fingers crossed he seems to be calming down. Although last week, after watching 'Snow White' he took some of my sleeping pills, broke them open and stuffed the powder into an apple. When he got into his class he said 'I've brought you an apple Miss.' His teacher was overwhelmed. By eleven o' clock I was sitting in the Head Teacher's office, with her asking Billy why he had done it. He replied, 'I wanted her to be kissed by a Prince because at her age the clock was ticking.'

The Fella Bella

He didn't?

Mo

He did. The best thing was though, the teacher who took her home was called Mark Prince. I've heard he has been kissing her every night for the last two weeks.

The Fella Bella

That's beautiful, the lucky cow. Why is it when I kiss a man they stay as a frog?

Mo

Bella love, you have just not kissed enough.

The Fella Bella

Believe me Mo, look at my lips, and you thought I was wearing green lippy. *(They all laugh)*

Mo

See you soon everyone.

All

Bye Mo

She walks out of the hairdressers and down the street.

The Reunited Wedding

Characters

Michael

The love child of the Duke and Mo – he is thirty years old and six feet tall. He is getting married to Jane and they have two young children, James and Lucy. Michael is a carpenter by trade and is liked by everyone.

Lady Bet

She is a woman in her eighties, small in size with grey hair and is the sister of the Duke.

Chauffeur

A short plump man in his sixties, working for the Duke as a Chauffeur. He has a criminal past.

Takeaway Ted

A small man who is around five foot in height and massively overweight for a man in his sixties.

Di Rhea

A tall slim woman in her early sixties. She likes to look immaculate in her appearance.

Luke Rhea

The son of 'Takeaway Ted' and Di Rhea. He is around six feet tall and has a rugby style body.

Mr & Mrs Farceit

Small people who are the parents of the bride. Both are in their fifties. Honest working class people.

Jane

A medium size woman who is the bride. She comes from a working class background

Setting

Mo's House
Inside a Bentley car, travelling through the countryside
Fircum Hall

The Reunited Wedding

A chauffeur driven Bentley car parks outside Mo's cottage. The chauffeur gets out of the car and walks up the path to Mo's door, where he knocks on the door, Mo opens the door.

Chauffeur

Good morning Mrs Moore, are you ready?

Mo

Please give me a couple of minutes.

Chauffeur

I'll take your case to the car. *(Mo passes him a small case)*

The chauffeur takes the case to the car, while Mo goes back inside to talk to Ron.

Mo

Now, you have my number. If anything happens just ring me.

Ron

I will.

Mo

Also can you pop down to the market and see is Billy is alright. Knowing that father of his, he will be working him like a slave.

Ron

Don't worry I'll pop down.

Mo

Also, don't forget to feed Tabatha. Put her biscuits on top of her food.

Ron

Isn't his Grace waiting for you?

Mo

He is and I can't keep him waiting.

She kisses Ron goodbye and walks to the car. She looks back to see Ron holding Tabatha and moving her paw in a wave. Mo wave back with a smile. She gets into the car.

The Duke

Good morning, Mrs Moore. Where have you come from, Australia?

Mo

I'm sorry your Grace, but there's always some last minute details to sort out.

The Duke

I've heard you have a child living with you, a boyfriend and a cat. I never thought you were a cat sort of person? They always say, everything comes to those who wait.

Mo

It does seem that way.

The Duke

I heard what you did for that dying woman. I hope you feel as proud of yourself as we all do.

Mo

Do you know, Your Grace, I couldn't feel any happier than I do now. I have a nine year old boy, a boyfriend and even a cat that I love very much. I do feel highly blessed.

The Duke

Do you know, you deserve to be blessed, as does our son who

at the age of thirty has gone on to be a young man who is caring, honest and hard-working. That's what your genes have given him. Let's not forget his beautiful looks, which he got from his mother.

Mo

Stop it Your Grace. What profession did he go into?

The Duke

Carpentry. He was always good with his hands.

Mo

That, he got from his father. His father was always good with his wood.

The Duke

You are too kind. He works for an MP of mine who sits in the cabinet. The MP had to go to the doctors the other day.

Mo

Did he?

The Duke

He did. He said, 'Doctor I've got a splinter up me'. The doctor said, 'I'm not surprised, you have had half the cabinet'.

Mo

Your Grace. *(They both begin to laugh)*

The Duke

Let's have another drink. What is the point of having a drinks cabinet in the car, if you don't use it?

Mo

But I've had two already.

The Duke

One more won't matter.

Mo

It was that one more that got me pregnant.

The Duke

Third time lucky then, cheers. Pickering *(chauffeur)*, how much longer will we be?

Pickering

About another ten minutes Your Grace.

Mo

(In a low voice) Has he been with you long?

The Duke

A good few years. Pick by name, pick by nature.

Mo

Nose?

The Duke

Pockets. They used to call him the Fagin of the North.

Mo

What made him step up?

The Duke

Well he was walking through a park one day and in the distance he could see a couple of young men walking ahead, so he thought he would go through the middle of them and do the barge movement, that way he could pickpocket both of them at the same time. Well everything was going fine until he got his hands stuck in both their pockets. He had forgotten to cut his nails and they got caught up in the lining.

Mo

That was bad luck.

The Duke

Even worse, the two men were off-duty officers. Well of course they arrested him there and then. But when Pickering has his hands in their pockets, he felt that both men had erections, which wouldn't have been a problem. Only that he had seen one of the men a week ago in McDonalds with his wife and children having a happy meal.

Mo

That's happiness for you, here to-gay, gone tomorrow.

The Duke

So of course they had to let him go. As they did, one of the officers said to him, it's only a matter of time before you get sent down for a long stretch. So he told him with his skills as a driver, he knew of someone who needed a chauffeur and here he is.

Mo

What made you take him on?

The Duke

I needed someone who could make quick getaways when a woman's husband came back unexpectedly. But touching those erections seemed to change his sexual preference. He has amazing oral skills. *(The Duke smiles)*

Mo

Your Grace, where is it we are going?

The Duke

Fircum Hall. Have you ever been?

Mo

Just the once. The guided tour.

Pickering

We have arrived Your Grace.

The Duke

Wonderful.

The chauffeur opens the door for the Duke, Mo follows behind. They walk into the entrance Hall, where they are met by Lord Fircum.

Lord Fircum

How wonderful it is to see you.

The Duke

You too. This is Mrs Moore, a dear friend of mine.

Lord Fircum

How nice to meet you. Do you know, your face seems familiar?

Mo

Does it? I'm afraid yours doesn't and it's a face you wouldn't forget.

Lord Fircum

Thank you for your compliment. My men will take you up to your rooms. At twelve we will be serving a light lunch in the dining room.

The Duke

Splendid. We will see you then. *(The Lord's servant takes them up to their rooms, where they find their clothes unpacked)* I will see you later Mrs Moore.

Mo

Thank you Your Grace.

At twelve o'clock the Duke knocks on Mo's door. Mo opens the door.

The Duke

Are you ready Mrs Moore?

Mo

I am Your Grace

The Duke

Then take my arm and I'll lead you down. *(As they descend the stairs, the Duke stops)* Have you seen these family portraits? The biggest lot of sluts, wasters and thieves you could ever wish to meet. Take these three for example. *(He points to each picture)* She was the mistress of the first Lord and married the second Lord. She married the fifth Lord and the servants as well. She was hired out to the highest bidder, in order to help pay off the sixth Lord's debts. What a family.

They arrive at the bottom of the stairs and walk into the dining room.

Lord Fircum

There you are. I'm sure Your Grace knows most of the people here, with the exception of the bride's parents. *(They both stand up)* Mr and Mrs Forceit.

The Duke

How nice to meet you both.

Mr Forceit

Likewise, Your Grace.

The Duke

What an unusual name.

Mr Forceit

Do you think so, Your Grace? It's a name that is appropriate.

The Duke

Is it?

Mr Forceit

It is. When we first met, Mrs Forceit forced me into bed. Then she forced me to give her intercourse. She has a high sexual appetite.

The Duke

Has she?

Mr Forceit

She definitely has. Then she got pregnant and so her parents forced me to marry her and when the baby came, she forced it out in less than five minutes. So you see, Your Grace, it's a very appropriate name.

The Duke

I can see that it is. Well, at least she won't be forcing any more babies out. Her clock stopped a long time ago.

Mo sits down next to the Duchess of Ruttingham.

The Duchess

Hello Mrs Moore.

Mo

Hello Mrs Ruttingham.

The Duchess

Call me Brenda.

Mo

Call me Mo. So how have things been going in the lower reaches?

The Duchess

Let's just say, it feels as if it's been on many a coach trip. In fact, it feels as though it's been around the world twice.

Mo

That good?

The Duchess

Bloody amazing.

Mo

How do you get away with it?

The Duchess

We have employed him as a part time gardener. Only trouble is he is always clipping my bushes and not those in the garden. *(They both laugh)*

Lord Fircum

Your Graces, ladies and gentlemen, with the wedding in less than two hours, I suggest we retire to our rooms to prepare.

As they all rise, the Duke of Ruttingham starts to sway.

Mo

Do you think he will last?

The Duchess

If it's anything like the bedroom, there's not a hope in Hell.

They all go up to their rooms with bottles in hand. At around three thirty, the Duke knocks on Mo's door. She opens it to reveal a two piece outfit with a wide brimmed hat.

The Duke

You look radiant my dear. An outfit that would make any son proud.

Mo

Thank you, Your Grace. What a handsome man you are.

The Duke takes Mo's arm and leads her towards the small Chapel at the side of the house. As they go down the aisle to their seats, the Duke whispers in Mo's ear.

The Duke

We could have gone down the aisle together over thirty years ago. I love you now as I loved you then. *(Mo smiles)*

As they reach the front row, Michael comes over to hug his father.

Michael

Hello father.

The Duke

This is Mrs Moore, a dear friend of mine.

Michael

How wonderful to meet you. (They shake hands)

Mo

It's a pleasure to meet you. (They stare at each other for a few seconds)

As the music begins, Mo goes to sit next to the Duke. As she sits, the lady next to her holds her hand.

Lady Bet

Hello.

As Mo sees who it is, she squeezes Lady Bet's hand. The wedding march starts to play and two small children throw petals on the floor. The bride is led down the aisle by her father. At the bottom of the aisle, he gives her hand to Michael and sits down with the children. As the vicar begins, a tear runs down Mo's cheek. Lady Bet leans over and whispers in Mo's ear.

Lady Bet

Those children are your grandchildren.

She shows a face of disbelief, with a trickle of tears becoming a flood.

Vicar

Now I pronounce you husband and wife. *(They both kiss)*

Everyone stands as they walk up the aisle. Outside they all pose for photographs. The photographer asks for the bride and groom, with their parents. The bride's parents line up on one side and the Duke stands next to Michael.

Michael

Mrs Moore would you stand next to me? *(Mo looking a bit shocked)*

Mo

I would love to.

After the photos are finished, Michael goes up to Mo.

Michael

Mrs Moore? (Mo turns around)

Mo

Yes Michael?

Michael
After the honeymoon, we are coming up for a weekend to visit my father. I wonder if I could pop round and see you?

Mo
Of course you can, you will be very welcome. *(Michael's son comes over)*

Michael
James, this is Mrs Moore.

Mo
Hello James, how old are you?

James
I'm five and my sister is four. We are going to visit Grandpa Cavendish very soon.

Mo
I'm sure you Grandpa is looking forward to your visit.

James
Can I come and see you?

Mo
That would be very nice and bring your Mummy and sister with you.

James
I will Mrs Moore.

Mo
I will see you very soon. Michael, you have a beautiful son. You enjoy the rest of your day.

Michael

Thank you Mrs Moore.

Mo walks away towards Lady Bet. She takes her arm as they both walk into the great hall for the reception as they sit down next to each other, the toastmaster introduces the Best Man.

Toastmaster

My Lords, Ladies and gentlemen, the Best Man.

The Best Man

Thank you very much. Now, I've been told to keep it brief due to the fact that some of our mature guests won't be able to hold it in for any length of time. That won't be any surprise, due to the fact of all the free champagne that is being consumed. *(Everyone says cheers and raises their glasses)* You will find Noah building his ark at the back of the hall. *(They all laugh)* What can I say about Michael that has not already been said? Kind, loyal and a great laugh on a night out. In fact, it's because of our holidays and hotel stays that Michael came into contact with wood. As he thought on many occasions that the wardrobe was the toilet. *(Everyone laughs)* That was one place you didn't hang your clothes. Before we toast the bride and groom, I have a few cards to read out. *(He opens the first card)* To Michael and Jane, you still owe us a tenner. Have a great day from Martin and Helen. *(He opens the next card)* To Michael and Jane, could you clean up the mess on my lawn, that has come from your dog's bottom. Have a wonderful life together, from Paul and Craig. *(The next card)* To Michael and Jane, could you return the toaster you borrowed four weeks ago. Have a wonderful day from Simon and Pat. Let's try one more. To Michael and Jane, have a wonderful wedding. Would have liked to be there but didn't get an invite. Love Pete and Tony. Please stand and raise your glasses to the bride and groom.

Everyone

The bride and groom.

Toastmaster

The Duke of Cavendish.

The Duke

Thank you. There are some pleasures in life that are so overwhelming you feel you are on top of the world. When you were born Michael, I was on top of the universe. You were a beautiful child who radiates so much love. As your father I couldn't have been more proud of you than I am today. Now I know you have become a skilled and dedicated carpenter, which for some time you have worked to set up on your own. Well, two weeks ago I secured a property for you, with everything in your name. So you can love your dream. *(Everyone applauds and a tearful Michael goes to hug his father. After the hug, Michael goes to sit down and his father continues)* But of course, to start up any business costs money, so here is a little money to help you on your way. *(He hands Michael an envelope. The Duke raises his glass)* To the bride and groom. *(Everyone stands up)*

Everyone

To the bride and groom.

Toastmaster

The groom.

Michael

(Holding his father's gift) I would first like to thank you all for coming. You have all made this day so much more special by being here. With my beautiful wife and wonderful children. I do feel as though I'm the luckiest guy on the planet. I know you must be starving by now, but I would just like to thank my wonderful father who has given me love and support all of my life. Thank you so much. Please raise your glasses to my father. *(Everyone raises their glasses)* Enjoy the rest of the day. *(When he finishes talking, he opens his father's envelope. He bursts into tears and collapses into his chair)*

Jane

Michael, what is it? *(He hands her the cheque)* Michael this is for a million pounds. *(She, too, bursts into tears. They both go over and hug the Duke)*

The Duke

That is your part of the estate Michael. Work hard and be successful.

As the amount circulated around the hall, gasps of disbelief can be heard. The food is brought out.

Mo

Well, you don't see that every day.

Lady Bet

True. But you don't see a father who loves his son that much every day.

Mo

Why was Michael his favourite?

Lady Bet

Because he came out of you. He loves you so much and would have done anything for you. I don't know if you knew, but he wanted to renounce his Dukedom and divorce his wife. But he knew the sacrifice would be too much. Due to your circumstances, he did insist that he would bring up Michael. Although the Duchess hated the idea, she knew she had no choice - mind you, she did mellow towards him as time went by.

Mo

I must thank you for letting me see him from time to time.

Lady Bet

The amount of times I saw you looking through the gates showed me the love you had for your baby.

Mo

Did you ever marry, Lady Bet?

Lady Bet

You know I did but it only lasted for about a year.

Mo

Why was that?

Lady Bet

I'm afraid my husband was never that well-endowed. So when we employed a new gardener, I thought this was my chance to have the orgasm I deserved. Trouble was the gardener was twice as small as my husband. How unlucky can you yet? My husband found out and threw me out. I had nothing. Luckily my brother took me in after a lot of pleading and begging. But I was always considered after that, the black sheep of the family, and even more so when I had an affair with the footman. They banished me to a small cottage in the lakes. But do you know, Mo? I didn't mind because the footman was hung like a donkey, giving me orgasms every time. So it was worth it.

Mo

I don't see Michael's brother and sister?

Lady Bet

You won't do. When you are as stuck up as they are and have two children out of wedlock, there isn't much chance of them attending. It was probably why Michael wanted his wedding at Fircum Hall. *(They both laugh)*

Mo

Do you know Lady Bet, its nine o'clock, where has the time gone?

Lady Bet

This disco music is a bit loud.

Mo

Bloody hell, how big is that man?

Lady Bet

That's 'Takeaway Ted', he is four in a bed. He is a descendent of the Lord Sandwich. Although a sandwich wouldn't touch the sides with that whale of a mouth.

Mo

Has he always been that size?

Lady Bet

He was half the size before he married but his wife won't cook. She says it would ruin her nails.

Takeaway Ted comes over to speak to Lady Bet.

Takeaway Ted

Lady Bet, it's been years since I've seen you. How are you?

Lady Bet

I am well thank you Mr Rhea. How's the family?

Takeaway Ted

They are doing find. Let me get Di to say hello. *(He walks off to find his wife)*

Mo

What's her first name?

Lady Bet

Yes you did hear it right, and believe me she is full of it. When she goes to the toilet she doesn't sit on it, she puts her big mouth over it. *(Takeaway Ted brings Di over)*

Di Rhea

Lady Bet, how wonderful to see you. You are looking so well, despite your isolation for so many years.

Lady Bet

What beautiful nails Mrs Rhea.

Di Rhea

You are too kind.

Lady Bet

Is that your son over there?

Di Rhea

It is, with his girlfriend Yvette.

Lady Bet

He has become a big strapping lad. I bet no one messes with him?

Di Rhea

It's all the sport he does. He loves his rugby and is never out of the gym. He is what you call a true man.

Lady Bet

Did I hear a rumble of thunder and see a flash of lightning?

Di Rhea

Well I didn't.

Lady Bet

There it is again.

They all look toward the buffet table where Luke Rhea is

standing. With another flash of lightning, they see that he is crying, followed by uncontrollable screaming, as high pitches as a girl. The music stops and everyone stares at Luke. He collapses onto the floor and crawls under the table. His girlfriend goes bright red with embarrassment and storms off. Di rushes over and gets on her hands and knees.

Di Rhea

Luke my little baby, mummy is here. Did the nasty thunder and lightning scare my little boy?

He comes out from under the table, and into his mother's arms.

Luke

Mummy tell the nasty thunder and lightning to go away.

Di Rhea

Come on my baby, let's get you home.

As they walk out of the hall everyone's eyes follow them, with their mouths open. Lady Bet and Mo are seen in hysterical laughter.

Lady Bet

I think there's more water under my chair than there is outside.

Mo

Lady Bet if I didn't know you better, I would have thought it was you who brought the lightning and thunder.

With the music back on, Samie the groovy granny takes to the floor.

Lady Bet

Bloody hell, not Samie the groovy granny.

Mo

How much makeup? How short is that skirt?

Lady Bet

You wouldn't think she was in her eighties. She had been many times a mistress. Trouble is, she has been many times the bridesmaid but never the bride. Because she loves sex so much, she has always looked at the size of the penis and not the size of the bank balance.

Mo

She has just touched up those two men. No wonder they don't look happy.

Two of Lord Fircum's servants come over and pick Samie up by the arms. This reveals her Union Jack underwear.

Lady Bet

Well I'll say on thing for her, she has always been patriotic. She always went with British men. Well my dear it's time for me to retire to bed. I've had a wonderful day and thank you for being such good company. Don't worry about Michael, he will be just fine. Good night my dear.

Mo

Good night Lady Bet and thank you.

They hug and Lady Bet walks out of the hall. Mo is seen sitting on her own looking out at the dance floor. Ron comes up behind her and whispers in Mo's ear.

Ron

I've heard there is a young lady who would like a dance.

Mo

(Turning around) Ron, what are you doing here?

Ron

I've told you, to dance with a beautiful lady.

He walks towards the dance floor, turns and holds out his hand. Mo gets up and holds his hand. Ron takes her to the dance floor where they are seen dancing close to each other to 'Lady in Red'.

We are the Champions

Characters

Judy

A tall, slim woman in her mid sixties. She is privately educated, so comes over as rather posh.

Brian

A small plump man in is early sixties. He wears thick rimmed glasses and is easily led by dominant women.

Matt

An overweight guy in his mid forties.

Johnny

A tall blond man in his early thirties. His youthful looks enable him to flirt successfully with women of all ages.

Flo

A small woman in her mid fifties although she looks and acts like a woman ten years older. She has an indecisive nature which gets on peoples nerves.

Lee O Lycra

A medium sized man in his late fifties. He overlooks much of the comments and innuendos to keep the show flowing.

Setting

A television studio.

We are the Champions

Lee O Lycra
Welcome everyone to another session of Poach Yolks. We are joined today by the Village People. Please introduce yourselves.

Harold I'm Harold
I'm fifty-five. I'm single and ready to mingle. *(Everyone laughs)*

Sarah Summers
(Looking at Harold) Fifty-five, of course you are.

Harold
What do you mean? What are you saying? What are you implying?

Sarah Summers
Fifty-five is nearer your weight than your age.

Harold
I'll have you know I've had this hour-glass figure for many years.

Sarah Summers
You want to try and clean the glass once in a while.

Harold
Bitch.

Lee O Lycra
Would you like to introduce yourself?

Sarah Summers
My name is Sarah. I'm fifty and I'm a carer in the community.

Harold

Fifty? A Carer? The only thing you care about is getting your house cleaned for free.

Mo

I'm Mo and unlike some, I like being my age of fifty- nine. *(Gasps from others. Mo sticks two fingers up)* I'm also a shoulder to cry on for the community. *(They all stand up and give Mo a hug)*

The Fella Bella

(Sitting down). I'm Bella. I'm just twenty-nine. *(Everyone shakes their heads)* I'm a top hair stylist and model. *(She stands up to reveal a figure-hugging dress)*

Penny Pick a Nose

I'm a mature lady who is not only a greater maker of cakes, but I'm planning to audition for The Great British Bake Off. *(Everyone groans)*

Lee O Lycra

Thank you all for your honesty. That's the Village People everyone. *(Everyone applauds)*

Sarah Summers

The only honest thing you need to know Lee is, when wearing lycra shorts, there's nowhere to hide. I put them on my smaller friends. That way they work harder to finish their jobs quicker. No one wants to cry of embarrassment for long. *(Sarah takes her coat off to reveal her dominatrix outfit)*

Lee O Lycra

(Stumbling with his words) As usual we will ask each contestant three questions, which if they get them right, they could find themselves in the final playing for ten thousands pounds. The first category is sport. Who would like to play first?

Sarah Summers

Don't look at me. The only sport I know is giving my clients a sporting chance of not receiving too much pain.

The Fella Bella

Well, with my firm, round breasts, the last time I did any sport I got two black eyes.

(They look at Penny and shake their heads)

Harold

I suppose it will have to be me.

Lee O Lycra

Who would you like to play against?

Harold

I think Judy. With her size, I'm sure she won't know much about sport.

Lee O Lycra

Harold and Judy, off you go to the question room. Harold do you want to go first or second?

Harold

I'm used to taking the lead, *(laughter)* so I'll go first.

Lee O Lycra

Harold which football team won the League Cup in 2018 and 2019? Was it Liverpool, Wolves or Manchester City?

Harold

I know this one. It's Manchester City. The players look better in shorts. That's why I watch them.

Lee O Lycra

Correct. Judy how many players are there in a women's netball team? Five, six or seven?

Mo

How easy is that?!

The Fella Bella

A primary school child could answer that question.

Judy

As I used to play in the England Under Eighteen's Team...

Sarah Summers

Snotty cow.

Judy

...The answer is six

Lee O Lycra

I am afraid it's seven.

Mo

Oh dear nobody wants to see that happen.

The Fella Bella

They say they're the best quiz team in the land. They must mean the little bit of land at the bottom of my garden that's full of weeds.

Lee O Lycra

Harold. Which city stages the start of the Tour de France? Manchester, Bristol or Leeds?

Harold

I'm not quite sure about this one. But many years ago I met a beautiful guy who had the most perfect body. In fact when he was naked I just wanted to put a picture frame around him and hang him on my bedroom wall. This guy came from Leeds, so I will say Leeds.

Lee O Lycra

Well I don't know how you do it, but that's correct. *(The team applaud)* Judy, let's see if we can get you on the score board.

Sarah Summers

A dart board would be best. *(They laugh)*

Lee O Lycra

Judy. How many times did John McEnroe win Wimbledon? One, two or three times?

Judy

I know this one, as I have been in the royal box many times.

Sarah Summers

The only box she needs to be in is a wooden one. *(They laugh)*

Judy

It's three.

Lee O Lycra

Correct. Harold get this question right and you're through to the final.

Mo

Come on Harold.

Lee O Lycra

Which of the major golf tournaments has Jack Nicklaus won the most times? Is is USPGA, Masters or the US Open?

Harold

Well again, I'm not too sure. But from time to time I do like a bit of S/M. Where a master ties me up and abuses my body, so I will say The Masters.

Lee O Lycra

Well it seems your sexual experiences have made you a winner. That's correct. *(The Village people all get up and start dancing to YMCA)* Well done Harold come and join us. Now who would like to play in the next round? The subject is History.

Sarah Summers

I'm ready and willing. *(She gets her whip out)*

Lee O Lycra

Who would you like to play against?

Sarah Summers

Definitely Brian. I'll whip him into shape. *(Brian is shaking with hot sweats)*

Lee O Lycra

Would you like to go first or second?

Sara Summers

First of course.

Lee O Lycra

How many of Henry VIII's wives were executed? One, two or three?

Sarah Summers

There were two heads that the axe fell on. We don't want a third do we Lee?

Lee O Lycra

(Hesitating) That's correct. Brian, which royal is fourth in line to the throne? William, George or Charlotte? *(Sara waves her whip)*

Brian

That would be Charlotte.

Lee O Lycra

That's correct. Sarah, what form of punishment was very popular in the fourteenth and fifteenth centuries? The rack, the grot or the thumb screw?

Sarah Summers

The rack. It's very popular in the twenty-first century at my place.

Lee Lycra

That's correct. Brian *(who is seen without his shirt on)* which year did Neville Chamberlain resign? 1939, 1940 or 1941 *(Sarah shows her whip)*

Brian

(With sweat pouring off him) 1940.

Lee O Lycra

That's correct. Sara, for a hatrick. When was the American Declaration of Independence signed? July 2nd, July 4th or August 2nd 1776?

Sara Summers

Do you know Lee my men friends don't do independence, but as my birthday is on the second of August, I'll say the second of August.

Lee O Lycra

Do you know Sara that was such a hard one.

Sarah Summers
They always are around me.

Lee O Lycra
You are correct. Brian, to stay in the round... *(Brian is seen with just his underpants on)*....Isador Straus who died as a passenger on board the Titanic, was a co-owner of which business? Macy's, Selfridges' or Bloomingdale's?

Brian
(Breathing heavily and looking at Sarah's breasts) Bloomingdale's.

Lee O Lycra
Sarah is he correct?

Sarah Summers
I would have chosen Macy's, as Macey Grey is one of my favourite singers.

Lee O Lycra
You would be correct.

(The music comes on and they dance to YMCA. Brian is seen bending over naked. He is simulating being whipped)

Harold
Well done team.

Lee O Lycra
Well Village people that's two you have in the final. The next category is food and drink.

(Penny Pick a Nose stands up)

Penny Pick a Nose

I'm ready.

Lee O Lycra

Who would you like to play with?

Penny Pick a Nose

Matt.

Lee O Lycra

Penny and Mat take your places. Penny I want to thank you for bringing in those beautiful cup cakes. I know that Matt had two of them, so they must have been good.

Harold

Not surprised with his size! They should call him "Fat Mat, I can get a bus up my crack"

(They all laugh)

Penny Pick a Nose

Thank you. Love to bake. Although I've not been baking much lately, due to a bad cold. *(She sneezes and green snot is seen running down her nose. She uses her fingers to wipe it away).*

Lee O Lycra

Penny. What colour wine do you traditionally have with beef? Red, White or Blue?

Penny Pick a Nose

Well, I like to have a Martini each evening so I will say Red.

Lee O Lycra

That's correct. Matt, which cheese is traditionally used for pizzas? Cheddar, Mozzarella or Stilton?

(The camera goes to Matt who is looking very pale with his mouth open, staring at Penny's running nose. He throws up and collapses on the floor)

Lee O Lycra
Well you don't see that every day. With Matt unable to carry on, Penny you have a by into the final.

(The music starts and the Village People are seen dancing to YMCA)

Harold
Just one more to go.

Lee O Lycra
The next category is the human body. *(The Fella Bell stands up and puts her foot on the chair revealing her legs)*

The Fella Bella
That's my call to arms.

Lee O Lycra
Who would you like to play with?

The Fella Bella
I would love to play with Johnny.

Lee O Lycra
Bella and Johnny off you to. Bella, do you want to go first or second?

The Fella Bella
I would like to go first, so I can go all the way.

Lee O Lycra
Nice. Your first question. How many teeth are there in the

human body in adult life? 30, 32 or 34?

The Fella Bella
(Looking at Johnny, she opens her mouth) 32

Lee O Lycra
Correct. Johnny what is the length of the average stomach, 24,cms 25cms or 26 cms?

Johnny
(Looking at Bella touching her breast) 25 inch, I mean 25 cms.

Lee O Lycra
Correct. Bella, what is the average blood pressure of a human being 120/70, 120/80 or 120/90?

The Fella Bella
The average pressure is 120/80 *(looking at Johnny)* but no man's blood pressure is average around me. *(Lee crosses his legs)*

Matt
She is going for it this time.

Lee O Lycra
Correct. You are very good.

The Fella Bella
Don't you forget it.

Lee O Lycra
Johnny what is the master gland of the body, pituitary, penis or the pelvis?

Johnny
(Looking at Bella parting her legs) The p..p..penis, no the pituitary

Lee O Lycra

I'm sorry, but I must take your first answer. Bella to win the round. Which is the largest bone in the human body? The femur, clavicle or the sternum?

The Fella Bella

That's the femur. But if a man is with me, it's a different story.

Lee O Lycra

That's correct.

(The music plays and they dance to YMCA)

Harold

We have done it!

Lee O Lycra

Well that's definitely a clean sweep. That just leaves Flo from the 'Poach Yolks'. Harold as the captain, do you want to go first or second?

Harold

As we have come first in every round we will go first.

Lee O Lycra

Playing for ten thousand pounds. What is the capital of Australia Canberra, Sidney or Brisbane?

Harold

I've been there. A young man invited me to a barbecue. He had so much meat. Canberra.

Lee O Lycra

Correct. Flo, what currency do they use in India? The rupee, the dollar or the shilling?

Flo

That's the...it's on the tip of my tongue, it's...it's.. the rupee.

Sara Summers

I bet she is a virgin and works in a tea shop. *(Everyone nods)*

Lee O Lycra

That's correct. The Village People. Pygmalion by George Bernard Shaw, was first staged in 1913, not in London, but in which city? Vienna, Chichester or Cairo? *(They all shakes their heads)*

The Fella Bella

I went to Vienna once and had wonderful sex, up a tree, to the music, Johann Bach. Then there was a member of the orchestra who insisted he brought his drum with him and didn't he bang it?

Everyone

Slut.

Harold

Well by the looks of it we only have Bella's sex life to go on, so we will say Vienna.

Lee O Lycra

That's correct.

Harold

Bloody hell, it's a good job you didn't get off with a flute player, you would never have remembered it.

Lee O Lycra

Flo, which Australian singer joined the judging panel of the Voice UK? Kylie Minogue, Natalie Imbruglia or Olivia Newton John?

Flo

I think I know this, or do I?

Sara Summers

Bloody hell, here she goes again. *(Everyone starts to yawn and pretend they are sleeping on each other's shoulders)*

Flo

Don't rush me. Is it Olivia or is it Kylie? I don't know. I'll say Kylie Minogue. We are the same age. *(Laughter can be heard from the Village People)*

Together

The same age?

Lee O Lycra

That's correct. Now Village People you could be one away from ten thousand pounds. Here we go. The brothers Kevin and Michael O'Hare, both born in Hull became leading performers and administrators in which field? Opera, ballet or acting?

Harold

Anyone had a sexual experience in or with any of them? I think he's got us now.

Penny Pick a Nose

Well I had ballet lessons once. But my teacher said her tree had less nobbly bits than my legs.

The Fella Bella

I went to the Ballet once to see 'Swan Lake'. The main male dance forgot to put his pad think, between his legs. His bits were all over the place.

Harold

Well as we can only relate to the ballet, we will say ballet.

Lee O Lycra

You are *(pause)* correct. *(Everyone starts to cheer)* Flo, to stop them, in 1992, which single became the first ever to occupy the UK number 1 spot in four different years? Do they know it's Christmas? Bohemian Rhapsody, or She Loves You?

Flo

Now you have got me. I don't really have a clue. *(Yawning sounds can be heard)* I'm just going to say it..She loves You.

Lee O Lycra

It was Bohemian Rhapsody. You have just won ten thousand pounds.

(The Village People stand up, cheering and waving their hands. They start to sing ' We are the Champions'. After a few lines of the song, they all come onto the floor and dance to YMCA. Brian is seen dancing in Speedos. Matt is seen kneeling down being sick, with Judy dancing and crying at the same time. Lee starts dancing in his lycra shorts, next to Sarah)

Sarah Summers

I told you there is nowhere to hide in lycra.

Returning Home

Characters

Mo, Michael, Jane, James and Lucy (their two children) Tabitha (the cat).

Setting

Mo's Home.

Returning Home

(Michael walks up Mo's garden path and knocks on the door. Mo opens the door.)

Mo

Hello Michael, what a wonderful surprise.

Michael

It's wonderful to see you too.

Mo

Come in. We will go through to the garden, especially as the weather is so good.

(They both go through to the garden, where Michael sits down on the bench)

Mo

Tea or coffee?

Michael

Coffee would be good.

(Mo goes off to make the coffee as Michael watches the cat chasing a bird. After a few minutes, Mo comes back with the coffee)

Mo

There we go. Help yourself to sugar and biscuits.

Michael

I've just been watching the cat chasing a bird.

Mo

That's Tabitha. She came to me with her kittens on Christmas Day. She was in a poor state. But as you can see she is back to full health. You never know what wildlife she will bring into the house next. The other night I had been watching one of those black and white Dracula films. The next minute she rushes in with a bat. It escaped her and was flying around the living room. Anyone would think I was the bride of Dracula. *(They both laugh)*. But I do love her. Now you haven't come here to hear about my horror stories. You have come here to find some answers. What is it you would like to know?

Michael

I suppose like any child who didn't grow up with his mother. Why did father bring me up and not my mother?

Mo

Your mother couldn't due to circumstances that she found herself in.

Michael

But were those circumstances that bad to give up your child?

Mo

Michael, my first marriage was a disaster. He was a prolific womaniser, who felt nothing when taking the rent or gas money to fund his nights out, leaving me to sit on my own in the dark, with my coat and scarf wrapped round me, trying to keep warm. He also had affairs with my mother and sister. After a year I couldn't stand it any more and left. Two nights I spent on a park bench, until the cold forced me to go back home. A home which had an abusive father and a down- trodden mother. So when my second husband came along, I jumped at the chance to marry him. No I didn't love him, but it gave me a way out of the constant arguments, that having an alcoholic father brought. Now don't get me wrong Michael, I might not have loved my second husband, but he was a good man. He provided a roof over my head and went to work everyday as a gardener on your grandfather's, then, you father's, estate. So I never had to sit in a freezing house, feeling hungry again. Believe me, if you ever have to go through that, you never want to go through it again. So everything was fine until one day I was walking through the grounds when I bumped into your father. Well, talk about love at first sight. I was sweating, my heart was pounding. I knew from the minute I saw him what love was. It was only a matter of days before we started an affair. Yes Michael he pressed every button. He awakened me. But to cut a long story short, I soon became pregnant with you. So now we were left with the problem of what to do. Never once did I think about having an abortion. But I knew my husband would never allow me to bring you into his home. Your father wanted to leave his wife, but he would have had to see the doors shutting in his face once the news got around. It would have killed him. Although he was a Duke, he was also a man. Yes, I loved him, but my life before had taught me never to trust a man again. So it was agreed that he would take you and give you a life of security. When you were born, to give you up was the hardest thing I ever had to do. The guilt has never left me. I took long walks around the estate each day, in the hope of seeing you. Your Aunt Bet would take you for walks, which gave me the change to hold you.

Michael

I remember.

Mo

But with your Aunt being banished to the Lakes and you being packed off to boarding school, I was lucky to see you once or twice a year. But never forget you were always in my heart and always will be. Did you enjoy your childhood.

Michael

Yes I did. I made some very good friends, who are still good friends today. But at home I must admit, apart from my father, there was never the love there. My brother and sister, although friendly at times, never showed any love. That was the same with my adoptive mother, although she did mellow in time. But I do agree with you, to be the son of a Duke opens many doors. Although I had a good childhood, I always felt there was something missing.

Mo

Michael, I can only say how sorry I am, but if things had been different, I would have kept you in a heart beat. *(Michael leans over and kisses Mo's cheek)*

Michael

All that matters now is, we must never lose each other again. *(They hug each other)*

As they are hugging, the door bell rings, with a tear in her eyes, Mo goes to answer the door. It is Jane and the children.

Mo

Hello everyone.

Jane

Hello Mrs Moore.

Mo

(Mo hugs Jane) You will find Daddy in the garden. *(The children rush off)* How are you?

Jane

I'm fine, although, I must admit these last few weeks have been exhausting.

Mo

How was the honeymoon?

Jane

It was wonderful. Although on our first week it was gay pride.

Well I could have walked around naked and I wouldn't have got a second glance, but Michael takes his top off and there's a hundred pairs of eyes staring at his body. I wouldn't have minded so much, but he was loving the attention. *(They walk into the garden)* I was saying, you were loving the attention.

Michael
What, from the gays?

Michael
Well just think of all the money you saved from not having to buy me a drink. But I will say one thing, they knew how to party.

Jane
But the second week, I did make sure he remembered how good a woman's body felt. In fact if I'm not mistaken, I think I'm pregnant.

Michael
Jane, that's wonderful. You never said anything. *(He gets up and hugs her)*

Jane
Well I'm still not sure, but the way we were at it, I wouldn't be surprised. I have an appointment next week with the doctor.

Mo
Well we will keep our fingers crossed.

Michael
We are going to have to go. We are having lunch with father. Then we must head home. I don't know when I will get back up to see you, what with sorting out a new business. But we've got each other's phone numbers, so we will be able to keep in touch. Come on you two say goodbye to Mrs Moore. *(They give Mo a kiss, then walk to the door)*

Jane

(Hugging Mo) I will give you a call next week to let you know of my results.

Mo

Make sure you do.

Michael

Thank you. *(Hugging each other. Michael walks down the path, turning to wave)*

Revenge is Sweet

Characters
Mo, Janice, Phoebe, Kevin, Large Lil, Big Bertha, Dirty Kath.

Setting
The Community Centre.

Revenge is Sweet

Mo enters Dirty Kath's Café

Mo

Bloody hell, what's that smell. *(She goes to sit with Phoebe and Janice)*

Phoebe

Dirty Kath has started to take washing in. She was saying, it's a bugger trying to get some of the underwear clean.

Mo

Well she need to buy better washing powder.

Phoebe

It's not that, it's the sort of stains she is finding. The girls upstairs are using everything, from custard to jam to keep their clients happy. One client likes jam roly poly. So he has jam smeared all over him. Another one, she was saying, likes to be covered in gravy. This is because he wants to better his suntan in Spain.

Mo

Why's that?

Phoebe

So he doesn't have any white bits showing.

Mo

Phoebe, you could make a fortune supplying all their client's needs. It's not as though they are going to complain about the goods being out-of-date.

Phoebe

I don't know what you mean. I'm meeting them tomorrow for a chat.

Janice

Is that Pervy Pete from Front Street?

Phoebe

Kath said ever since she has taken washing in, Pervy Pete can't stay away. She said to me, "You know when fishermen haul their catch in, then throw some of the catch back for the seagulls?" I said "Yes". Well, she said, "That's what I do with Pervy Pete, I throw a pair of knickers at him". As she says, "It keeps him here buying".

(Kath walks up the café and gives Mo a piece of her cake)

Kath

This is a little present to thank you for what you did for poor Vee.

Mo

That's so kind of you.

Phoebe

I say Kath, did you have a death here last week?

Kath

You heard about that did you?

Phoebe

I did. What happened.

Kath

Well one of my regulars, Phil, who is always in trouble with the Old Bill, ordered the spaghetti bolognese and being a regular I thought I'd give him extra bolognese. Well, I just went to unload Carol's washing, when one of her bras fell onto the floor. Well for Pervy Pete on Front Street, he thought Christmas had come early. He was straight down on the floor and grabbed the bra. But luckily, I snatched it away from him, due to the fact the bra was so big. Anyway while this was going on, Phil, who is always in trouble with the Old Bill, was bitten by a mosquito and collapsed with his head in the spaghetti bolognese and because he had extra bolognese, he drowned. It was a terrible accident. Even today, I can't for the life of me, think how a mosquito had got into the café. Especially as I've always kept it so clean.

Phoebe

You do Kath.

Kath

You enjoy your cake Mo. I want to see you eat every last piece. *(Kath walks back to her counter)*

Mo

Do you know Phoebe Dickson, there are times I just don't know which face I'm talking to with you.

Phoebe

I don't know what you mean Mrs Moore Now eat your cake. You don't want to upset Kath do you?

Mo

If I eat this, I know I'm going to be throwing up for most of the night.

Phoebe

There's always a silver lining. Just thing how much weight you will lose.

Janice

Why are those people in bee hive suits. She hasn't got any bees has she?

Mo

No there's no pollen in mushrooms and mould. What it will be is, they are regulars and with prescription charges at nine pounds, it is cheaper to buy a suit than forking out on a prescription.

Phoebe

Anyway, why were you late meeting?

Mo

There was something I had to do at the Community Centre.

Phoebe

Now you have eaten your last piece of cake, let's get off. I will make a change to get there on time.

(Waving to Kath, they walk out of the café and down the High Street to the Community Centre. They are the first to arrive)

Kevin

Well this is a first. I would like to think you have arrived first because you have lost weight and can move more quickly. But looking at you, there's not much chance of that.

Janice

(Whispered) Vile.

(All the other people are now walking in)

Kevin

Come on I've not got all night. My dream is to see you all jogging in tracksuits and trainers, not shuffling in leggings, because that's the only item of clothing you can fit into. I bet you don't shuffle to the chip shop.

Janice

(Whispering) So vile.

Kevin

Now we are all here and the cranes have retreated, I have a couple of notices for you. Firstly, the Fat Fine doesn't seem to be working, at the level it is set. So I'm raising it to three pounds for every pound gained. This way it will stop you buying those two for one offers on chocolate and crisps. Why don't you pay a visit to Dirty Kath's café. That way you will always throw up what you eat. Another reason for the price rise is, I'm off for a week in the South of France. You know how expensive it is there. You all want me to have a good time, don't you?

Everyone

Yes.

Kevin

My second notice is, we are now on our second weighing machine and it's only April. So if you bust this one like you did the last one, I will be putting your subscriptions up to pay for a new one. So I suggest you look at yourselves, through a full length mirror each day. This will scare you into losing some weight. It horrifies me to see you with clothes on, so I would hate to think what it does to you to see yourselves naked. Come on then Lillian, let's get this horror show started. *(Lillian stands on the scales).* Sixteen stone three pounds. Bloody hell! You have lost five pounds. Have you been feeling ill or have they shut down all the food joints?

Large Lil

That's fifteen pounds you owe me. *(In an American accent)* See me at the end. Sucker. *(Everyone applauds her)*

Kevin

Well it looks like miracles do happen. Come on Bertha, there's not much chance of you losing any weight, especially with a new chip shop opening up on your road. *(Bertha walks up and stands on the scales).* Eighteen stone dead. Bloody hell! Have the fast food places made their doors smaller so you couldn't get in?

Big Bertha

That's thirty quid you owe me, Tosser. See you at the end. *(Everyone applauds her)*

Kevin

Now as you know we usually have Big Stella now, but as she is still in rehab for her anorexia *(Kevin bursts out laughing)* she, of course, is not here. She did text me to say, however, that she was hoping to make next month's meeting, as she has lost eight stone. I had just two words for, "You're bared". *(Everyone starts booing and shouting 'Tight Git')* Janice, get yourself up here. It's good to have someone who is constantly fat. *(Janice stands on the scales).* Sixteen stone five pounds. That's a loss of five pounds. For you to lose that amount, when you are always cramming burgers, chips and crisps in your oversize mouth, there has to be something wrong with these scales.

Janice

That's twenty-one pounds you owe me. See me at the end, Twat.

Kevin

I'm going to have to cut short the session, due to mechanical failure. We have more takeaway places to the mile in this area, so there scales must have had it. I would like also to thank you for ruining my trip to the South of France. If anyone deserves that trip, it is me. With my kind and helpful nature, I should be allowed to go. I hope you are all proud of yourselves and before you say it Bertha, the fruit and veg prize goes to Mo. *(Everyone applauds).* You will find some nice pears in the basket, Mo, unlike your own pair which has seen better days. I will see you all next month. Open the doors and bring in the cranes.

Janice

(As they are walking out) Now I know why you were late. You tampered with those scales didn't you?

Mo

I don't know what you mean. *(All three laugh)*

A Special Day

Characters

Satan Sue

In her early seventies. She is of medium size, with a very pale face, she wears a lot of black make up and has long black hair. She is a follower of all things dark and frightening and is the mother of Dick.

Stick Thin Finn

A six foot tall man in his forties. In his youth he was very thin, but now he has filled out more. He is Dick's best man.

Other Characters

Mo, Phoebe, Janice, Brenda and Dick, Penny, Pissed-up Pete.

Setting

The Church.

The Queen's Head.

A Special Day

Mo and Brenda get out of a Rolls Royce and walk up to the church door arm in arm

Mo

Well Brenda you look so beautiful and so happy.

Brenda

Do you know Mo, I am very happy. I've got a man who I love and two children I adore. I know now why they say life begins at forty. *(The sun comes out from behind a cloud)*

Mo

That sunlight is from your Mother. She is lighting up the way.

Brenda

Do you know Mo. I do miss her. I would have loved her to be here today.

Mo

Brenda, your mother is firmly in your heart, so she is always with you, wherever you are. *(They hug)* Now it's your last opportunity to say no. No one will think bad of you if you want to back down.

Brenda

No one will think bad about me! What in this village. I would be hung, drawn and quartered. The village gossips would have a field day for years.

Mo

I want you to be doing the right thing.

Brenda

Mo, you are so wonderful how you look after me and the others, but I am a hundred percent doing the right thing.

Mo

Then take my arm, we are going in. *(Laughing)*

Both ladies go through the church door. They are met by Brenda's children, Tommy and Jenny and their brother and sister Mary and Billy. The girls are wearing bridesmaid dresses. The boys are page boys. The wedding music begins and Brenda and Mo are seen walking down the aisle with Jenny, Tommy, Billy and Mary following. When they reach the altar, Mo sees the vicar is Piss-up Pete who likes it neat. Mo gives him an icy stare. She sits down with the children

Mo

(Whispering to Phoebe) If he makes one mistake, I'll kill him. *(She crosses herself)*

Phoebe

(Whispering) He's on the wagon.

Mo

What's on the wagon with him, I would like to know?

Piss-up Pete conducts the wedding without any hitches. Although halfway through, he is seen swaying, with Mo's icy stare to stop himself

Piss-up Pete

I now pronounce you husband and wife. You may kiss the bride. *(Everyone in the church applauds)*

They both walk up the aisle to the church door, where a photographer is waiting for them

Photographer

Can I have the immediate family of the bride and groom please?

Brenda

Come on Mo.

Mo goes over to stand next to Brenda and Dick's mother, Satan Sue stands next to Dick, with the two children at the front

Photographer

Right, everybody in. *(They all have their picture taken)*

Stick Thin Finn

Ladies and gentlemen, if you would all like to walk down to the Queen's Head, you will find the buffet is open.

They all start to walk down to the Queen's Head

Phoebe

She looks just as scary as I remember her. Where is she living now?

Mo

Somewhere in the west.

Phoebe

I didn't see her in the church.

Mo

You wouldn't have done, too many crosses. If she had got some of the holy water on her, it would have burnt her like acid. She can't deal with the light, hence the dark glasses.

Janice

Bloody hell is she that bad?

Mo

Witchcraft, devil worshipping, even black magic. They say she killed her third husband by voodoo. Mind you, seeing as he was bi-sexual, I bet he didn't think it would be that sort of a prick that would kill him. *(They all laugh)*

Janice

What started her off like this?

Mo

Well apparently, when she was young, she was in a Dracula film. She played the part of a young virgin, which was a big of a joke, seeing that everyone at school used to call her 'Put out Sue'. Anyway as Dracula went to bite her neck, she slapped him over the face, then bit his neck. He lost two pints of blood and had to be rushed to the hospital. It's not everyday you see Dracula at A&E being given blood freely. From then on she stayed on the dark side.

Janice

What a way to live.

(They all arrive at the Queen's Head)

Harold

Come in everyone, the buffet's open. Penny, *(everyone freezes)* can you go and sit down away from the buffet. We don't want you sneezing over the food. *(Everyone starts moving and talking again)*

Everyone helps themselves and sits down to eat their food. Dick and Brenda walk through the door

Stick Thin Finn

(On the stage) Please raise you glasses to the bride and groom.

Everyone

The bride and groom.

Phoebe

Finn looks as if he has filled out a bit. Didn't he used to work at the Manor for a time?

Mo

He did, but he was always hungry, even to the point where the cook had to put the Duke and Duchess on rations. Mind you, they got away with it for about six months, until the Duke lost half a stone. When the Duke confronted the cook, she spilled the beans. That was the end of Finn.

Phoebe

Why ever he moved in with that whale of a girlfriend of his, I will never know. There was never anything in their cupboards. The local chippy had to take on extra staff to cope with her orders. Is he still with her?

Mo

No. Didn't you hear? She died.

Phoebe

Did she? What of?

Mo

Over-eating. Well what happened was, she put her usual order in at the chippy. Double pie, large chips, four fish cakes and a large tub of peas. Of course, they had to deliver it. She would never had made it down the road. In fact, she had been known to catch a taxi and it was only a two minute walk from her place. Anyway she scoffed all that down her, when just as she had finished, there was a knock at the door. It was the pizza boy with two large pizzas with extra topping. She had forgotten she had ordered them half an hour before.

Phoebe

What did she do?

Mo

Well as you know, she could never say no to food. So when she had eaten the first one, she started to get chest pains. Next minute she keeled over with her face smack down in the second pizza. When the ambulance came, the ambulance man said, "If she hadn't had extra topping she would've survived."

Phoebe

Why?

Mo

It was the extra topping that suffocated her.

Phoebe

Poor cow. What a way to go.

Stick Thin Finn

Ladies and gentlemen, as the best man, I would firstly like to read out some greetings cards for the happy couple. The first one: Could you pay off your slate of six pounds before we send round the bailiffs. That from all of you friends at the Offy. The next one: To Dick and Brenda, if you get too many toasters bought you, would you mind if we could have one? That fool of a husband of mine blew up the last one, because he thought sausages would cook faster in a toaster. I kicked his sausage all around the kitchen. Love Carol and Tony. The next one: Congratulations to both. I forgot to tell you Brenda our prices have gone up, so you owe five pounds. From all your friends at Blow and Go. Let's try one more. Congratulations to you both. As a wedding present, I'm giving Dick a free afternoon in my dungeon. Love Sarah. It's so nice to read so many kind words that congratulate you on your special day. What can I say about Dick that has not already been said? Dick was a creature of hab-it. You always knew where to find him if you wanted a night out.

What a true friend. Even if he had passed out and was on his way to hospital, a few coins would always fall out of his pocket, so you could get yourself a drink. What a true friend. The next night when he couldn't remember a thing from the night before, he was back in the pub giving his friends advice on what drinks were best for staying sober for longer. What a true friend. Please raise your glasses – the bride and groom.

Everyone

The bride and groom.

Dick

Thank you Finn for those kind words. It's good that you can remember these happy times, because I can't remember a bloody thing *(everybody laughs)*. But I do remember the kindness and love that the people in this village have shown. A year ago I didn't have any family to speak of, but now I have a beautiful wife and two wonderful children. Believe me, life is amazing-thank you Brenda so much, for saying Yes. Raise your glasses to the bride everyone.

Everyone

To the bride.

Dick

Thank you to those who organised the buffet and for a wonderful cake. Thank you so much P...*(everyone stands like a statue with no talking)*...at. *(everyone cheers)*. Before I cut the cake with my beautiful wife *(everyone claps)* I have a gift here, for a woman who I can say is truly a living saint. Who if it wasn't for her, we would not have two beautiful children today. We both love you so much and we are so grateful that you are in our lives now and for always. Mo everyone. *(As Mo walks up to the stage everyone stands and applauds. Dick gives her a hug)*

Mo

Thank you both. When I took on the responsibility to find new families for Vee's children, you both were at the top of my list. I know any child coming into your home would be so loved and cared for. You're both are so deserving. So I wish you all, as a family, good health and much love. *(Raising her glass)* To the family.

Everyone

(Standing) To the family.

(After the toast, Dick and Brenda go to cut the cake. Afterwards they hand the cake out to all their guests)

Dennis

(Going up onto the stage) Could I have your attention please? I do hope the bride and groom will forgive me for making an announcement, but next Wednesday a coach will be arriving outside the Queen's Head at ten in the morning. It's to take anyone who would like to go to the Antiques Roadshow, which is taking place at Windy Pier. Those who do want to come, you are allowed to bring no more than two antiques, because of the space on the coach. Although looking at some of you, I think it will be best to just bring yourself. *(He starts to laugh, but everyone else is silent)*

Phoebe

I walked along Windy Pier once. My dress flew right up.

Mo

I bet it did and there was no wind. Slut. *(They all laugh)*

Janice

Where is everyone this evening?

Mo

Well Gemma rhoids, had her haemorrhoids taken out yesterday. She has been rolling around her bed in agony. Donna has been rolling with her in order to put cream on her bottom.

Phoebe
Doesn't bare thinking about.

Mo
Carol and Tony aren't here because Carol hasn't any bras to wear.

Phoebe
They haven't got bigger?

Mo
No Tony forgot to get any hanging baskets, so he thought he would use Carol's bras instead. When she got up in the morning, she found Tony posing for photos next to his handy work.

Phoebe
Did she kill him?

Mo
Let's just say he spent two hours in A&E. Pill Gill has gone to her sister's.

Phoebe
Why's that?

Mo
Well she was taking her usual six thousand tables, when she accidentally swallowed a couple of Es that got mixed in with her usual tablets. Next minute she is Wonder Woman, trying to fly out of her bedroom window. So they packed her off to her sister's. She lives in a bungalow.

Phoebe
Bless her.

Harold
Well it's that time again. I hope you all have got your cards for a

chance to win some fabulous prizes.

Mo

Come on Brenda, get yourself sat down over here. I've got your card.

Brenda

I can't play bingo on my wedding day.

Mo

Of course you can. Especially as its your big day.

Harold

Here we go, number 1, Gemma's got a sore bum *(laughter)*. Number 4, is Dennis dogging once more? *(Laughter)*. Number 21, just my age.

Mo

You wish.

Harold

Number 10, Gills flying again.

Dennis

Yes

Harold

Come on Dennis let's see what you have won. A twenty pound gift voucher for Pete's Pet Shop.

Dennis

Wonderful, but I don't have any pets.

Harold

I hear you are a bit of an animal Dennis. You can buy yourself a dog collar, for your outing.

Dennis

I don't know what you mean. *(Everyone starts to make dog noises)*. You are all barking. *(Everyone cheers. Dennis walks off the stage)*

Harold

Now for a full house everyone. Number 88 – Carol's tits over her place *(laughter)*. Number 10 Sarah's Den. Number 69, Mo has come alive *(laughter)*. Number 6 Finn doesn't look like a stick. Number 25, Brenda's going to eat Dick alive.

Brenda

Bingo!

Harold

It's certainly your lucky day today. Come up Brenda and bring your husband with you. *(They both walk onto the stage)* Well now, let's see what you have won. It says here at six o'clock tomorrow morning a taxi will pick you up and drive you to the airport. You will fly off to Paris for three night at the Hotel Mercury. You first day will be touring Paris, visiting all the beautiful sights. Then on the next day you will be off on an excursion to The Palace of Versailles. I told you, play Harold's bingo and you can see the world.

Brenda

(With tears in her eyes) Thank you so much. You all are truly wonderful people. But we can't go without passports and I can't leave my children on their own.

Mo

(Walking on the stage). I can solve your problems. Here are your passports and I'm looking after your children. My wedding present to you both. *(They both hug Mo)*

Harold

One last thing, Dick and Brenda, you need to have your first dance together as husband and wife.

Lady in Red starts to play. Dick and Brenda are seen dancing together. After a few seconds Ron comes through the door

Ron

(To Mo) I think they are playing our song. *(They both start to dance)*

Mo

(After the song) Right you two, you have an early start. The taxi has just pulled up. Come on everyone, let's see the bride and groom off.

They all follow Brenda and Dick out of the door, where they see a taxi which has been trimmed up. After their goodbyes, the taxi is seen driving away with the noise of tins on the back of the taxi

Mo

I bet you supplied the tins. That's one way to get rid of out-of-date stock.

Phoebe

How rude.

Ron

Right young lady, it's way past these children's bedtime.

Mo

Is that the time already. Girls, I'll see you both on the coach next Wednesday. Just bring yourselves. You are living antiques.

Phoebe/Janice

We don't know what you mean. *(They all fall about laughing)*

The Roadshow to Success

Characters

Expert 1

A small man in his sixties. He is obsessed by women's breasts.

Expert 2

A medium sized man in his later fifties.

Expert 3

A tall slender man in his early fifties. He is very professional in what he does.

The other Characters

Mo, Phoebe, Janice, Sarah, Denis, Harold, Mary, Carol and Tony, Vera Virus, Dog Face Dona, Emma rhoid and The Fella Bella.

Setting

On the coach
At the roadshow

The Roadshow to Success

Dennis

Morning Ladies.

Mo

Morning Dennis.

Dennis

Nice day for it?

Mo

A nice day for what?

Dennis

A nice day for showing your bits to an expert.

Mo

The only expert I show me bits to is a doctor. Who do you show your bits to, a vet?

All three get onto the coach. They sit in the middle, with Mo sitting next to Phoebe and Janice sitting behind

Phoebe

You would think they would clean the windows.

Mo

I heard they are going to be gleaming soon.

Janice

Why's that?

Mo

Sarah Summers has just secured the contract. Her clients, when they heard what was expected of them, went into orgasmic mode. She is teaching them the Wheels on the Bus song, with all of the actions. But the bit of the song where they sing ... "The driver on the bus says..." She has changed the words.

Phoebe

What to?

Mo

(Singing) "The driver on the bus says , "Yes Mistress, Yes Mistress, Yes Mistress", the driver on the bus says "Yes Mistress, all whipping long".

Phoebe

I'll say one thing for Sarah, she gives so much to her boys.

Mo

I was just thinking, the last time I was on a coach with you two, we all ended up on the floor, with a transexual copper talking about his sex life.

Phoebe

Have you seen him lately?

Mo

It's funny you should say that. The other day he was arresting someone who had just robbed the bank. He gave the bloke a good slapping.

Janice

Was that because he had just robbed the bank?

Mo

No it was because he was wearing a cheese cloth shirt. Mickey thought a shirt like that gave bank robbers a bad name. Anyway, as he has got him on the floor with his foot in his back, he was telling me it's his mum's birthday next Friday and she's having a party at the Laughing Cow. Mickey is performing.

Phoebe
Are you going?

Mo
We are.

Janice
I can't make it.

Mo
What are you doing a week on Friday?

Janice
It's our Luke's birthday and I'm doing the cooking.

Mo
Didn't you nearly burn the house down last time your cooked?

Janice
That wasn't my fault.

Mo
Whose fault was it?

Janice
The television.

Mo
How do you make that out?

Janice

I couldn't stop watching that new series on Saturday night.

Mo

What series is that?

Janice

London's Burning.

Mo

She gets worse. Your coming Phoebe?

Phoebe

Well, I'm down to do Saturday morning at the shop, but they owe me a favour or two, so put me down.

Mo

What have you brought with you?

Phoebe

Well, I looked all over the house, but could I find anything? Then I remembered, I had an antique in the bedroom.

Mo

Just the one?

Phoebe

I don't know what you mean.

Mo

Talking about men, are you still on that dating site?

Phoebe

Mo, it's like a magnet. It keeps drawing me in.

Mo

Of course it does. So have you met anyone?

Phoebe

I've met two, but I don't know who is choose.

Mo

Which one do you like best?

Phoebe

Well, they have both got qualities I like. There's Steady Eddy, who's sixty five and says he is kind and loving. Then there's Steve, who is thirty and has got two more years to serve of a ten year sentence.

Mo

What did he get locked up for?

Phoebe

For robbing his girlfriend. She wouldn't do the doggy position, which is not a problem for me.

Mo

Let's face it, no position is a problem for you. But I think you should play it safe with Steady Eddy.

Phoebe

I know what you mean. Have you seen Steven's profile pictures? *(Mo takes a look)*

Mo

You have got to be joking. That is the Dick of Death.

Phoebe

I know and my batteries are flat.

Mo

Well, you have got two years to think about it. So what have you brought?

Phoebe

As I was saying, I found my grandmother's old tea pot in the bedroom cupboard. With it's age, it must be worth a couple of quid.

Mo

You never know. Janice, what have you brought?

Janice

Well, it's an African club that has been passed down through the family for generations.

Mo

That looks gruesome.

Janice

That's what my grandfather said when he came home drunk one night from a Night Club. My Grandmother hit him with it, saying I've got the best club in town.

Mo

I'm surprised there was any generations left to pass it down. It's the sort of thing Sarah would love. Talk of the devil, here she comes. Morning Sarah!

Sarah

Morning Mo, Ladies.

Mo

What have you brought?

Sarah

Well, it was a toss up between a medieval mace or the rack.

Mo

You brought the rack.

Sarah

I thought it would be better in helping with recruitment. See you later.

Mo

That's one way of boosting profits.

Carol and Tony get on the bus

Carol

Hi Everyone!

Mo

Hi Carol. What have you brought?

Carol

Well, I've brought two things. Firstly, I've brought this old pot, which I've never liked. In fact every time I throw it away, Twat Face here gets it back out of the bin. So when they tell me it's worth nothing, I'm going to throw it in the bin with him after it.

Mo

What's the other thing?

Carol

It's my cup and saucer, that I drink from every day. I want to prove to him that it is a rare seventeenth century cup that is worth thousands.

Mo

Good luck with that. While I remember, do you fancy going out next Friday night? It's Sheila Ore's birthday in the Laughing Cow.

Carol

I'm in. Give me a ring with the details. See you in a bit love.

Next to come onto the coach is The Fella Bella

The Fella Bella
Hiya girls!

Mo
Hello love. What have you brought?

The Fella Bella
Underwear.

Mo
What, from the market?

The Fella Bella
No love. I went to a charity shop and bought some Mary Quant underwear.

Mo
Where are they?

The Fella Bella
(She lifts up her skirt) I've got them on.

Mo
Very nice. What does it say on the back?

The Fella Bella
"Virgins want to have fun"

Mo
Really, with that writing on the back, do you feel comfortable in them?

The Fella Bella
They hold everything beautifully.

Mo

Not everyone would get away with it.

The Fella Bella

What you trying to say, love?

Mo

I'm saying, are you free next Friday night. It's girls' night out at the Laughing Cow.

The Fella Bella

Put me down love. This cow can laugh with the best of them. *(She goes to sit down)*

Harold and Mary get onto the bus next

Harold

Hello you lot. Looking at you antiques, you're priceless.

Phoebe

What have you brought Harold?

Harold

I've brought a diamond ring, which one of my old boyfriends bought me.

Mo

That's beautiful Harold. Why did he buy you that?

Harold

Well, we went out to a beautiful restaurant that was inside a stately home. After the meal we went for a walk in the grounds, with just the moon for light. Next minute, he goes down on one knee and says will you marry me. Holding up this diamond ring.

Mo

What did you say?

Harold

Well I was just about to say yes, when there was this terrible smell which was so bad, I started to heave.

Mo

What was it?

Harold

When he went down on one knee, he knelt in a pile of dog muck. He was so embarrassed, he ran off. I never saw him again. But I did keep the ring.

Mo

You should have ran after him.

Harold

What do you think I am, a bloody greyhound? *(They all laugh)* Mary, tell Auntie Mo your good news.

Mary

I got three A Stars.

Mo

Mary that is wonderful. Congratulations. Everyone, Mary has passed her A levels. *(Everyone gets up and goes to hug Mary)* So what's your next step?

Mary

Well I have been offered a place at Oxford, but I need to go to work for a year, so that I can save up.

Mo

But you would like to go in September, wouldn't you?

Mary

I would, but......

Mo

No buts, Mary. Phone them up and accept the place they have given you for this year.

Mary

But Auntie Mo, I can't afford it.

Mo

Don't worry about the cost. Me and your Uncle Harold will sort it.

Mary

(In tears) Thank you so much. *(She hugs Mo and Harold together)*

They both sit down. Next to get on the coach is Dog Face Donna and Gemma rhoid

Mo

Hello girls.

Donna

Hello Mo.

Mo

How are you Gemma?

Gemma

Much better now. It was so painful. I didn't think I would survive. I was leaking all over the place. But Donna kept fingering my bottom with some antibiotic cream. In time the pain started to ease.

Mo

Donna, What you do for love! *(They both sit down)*

Dennis

Right everyone, belt up.

Harold

Who's he talking to?

Mo

Seat belts Harold.

Harold

That's a relief. I've got my elasticated trousers on. So I don't need a belt.

As the coach starts to go, Vera Viruse can be seen running beside the coach

Phoebe

Hold on driver, Usain Bolt is here. *(The coach stops and Vera, out of breath, gets on the coach)*

Vera Viruse

Sorry I'm late everyone, but Big Head May, got her head stuck under the drier.

Mo

She didn't!

Vera Viruse

She did. I had to call the Fire Brigade to get her out. It took them an hour. When they managed it, she came out looking like Friar Tuck. An ambulance took her to A & E.

Dennis

Ready when you are Driver.

The coach pulls off. Ten minutes later they are passing the local dogging area

Mo

(To Janice) Go and ask him.

Janice

Dennis *(in a loud voice)* why are there lots of cars parked up over there?

Dennis

Not as it's a place I know, but I heard that it's a good place to walk your dog.

Mo

Is that the human or animal type? *(Everyone bursts out laughing and starts barking)*

Dennis

Thank you everyone. Before we get there can I remind everyone, to please be careful when moving around. We don't want you to bump into any old relics.

Mo

Don't forget Phoebe.

Phoebe

Don't worry, not even Brillo pads could get the rust off that one *(talking about Dennis)*. Who needs cocktail sausages when you can get a full length sausage.

Mo

Phoebe you sound like a porn star.

Phoebe

Watch me next Friday night.

Dennis

Right everyone, we are just arriving. Please remember the coach leaves at two.

As the coach stops, everyone gets off holding their antiques

Mo

I think we need to get in the right queue.

They all wander off and stand in the right queues. Mo and Phoebe reach the expert's table

Expert 1

Now then ladies, what have you brought with you today?

Mo

We have brought two tea pots.

Expert 1

They do look a beautiful pair.

Phoebe

What looks a beautiful pair?

Expert 1

The teapots of course. Can you tell me about yours. *(He keeps looking at Phoebe's cleavage)*

Phoebe

Well it used to belong to my grandmother. She used it everyday. I think it was bought as a wedding present. It was handed down to my mother, then to me. I only use it in the mornings.

Mo

I bet you do.

Expert 1

Would you like to tell me about yours?

Mo

Well it's very much the same sort of story. Only that I don't think it was new when my grandmother had it.

Expert 1

You would be right. You would have to go back another two hundred years. This was made in the middle of the 17th Century. It's small size reflects how expensive tea was in those days. As opposed to your pot, which is huge. This was a reflection on how much the price of tea had dropped. Your pot was made around 1850. The mid Victorian period. Both are made from porcelain. Now the price. For a large Victorian teapot, between seven and nine hundred pounds. A rare 17th Century teapot, between two and three thousand pounds.

Mo

That's amazing.

Expert 1

It just shows you, size is not always the main factor.

Phoebe

You speak for yourself.

The next to see Expert 1 are Carol and Tony

Expert 1

Now what have you brought me? *(The expert can't take his eyes off Carol's breasts)*

Carol

First, every morning my husband brings me a cup of tea in bed. This is the cup he brings it in. This is a vase that my husband has brought. He thinks it's more valuable than my china cup and saucer.

Expert 1

I sense *(there is silence as the expert stares at Carol's breast. It lasts for a few seconds)* you don't like the vase.

Carol

I hate it. I've thrown it out twice, but he keeps taking it out of the bin.

Expert 1

Let's look at the cup and saucer that your husband brings your tea in every morning. It's styled on a china cup and saucer of the 16th century. Now if it was the 16th century the flowers and birds you can see on the side of the cup would have been hand painted. The decoration on this cup is transfer printed. This puts it to the early 20th century. Now if we look at the vase, which you hate so much. On the bottom of the pot we can see the name Moorcroft. The way the signature is written, tells us its a very early piece. So let's come to values. Your cup and saucer – thirty to forty pounds. The vase you hate – five thousand pounds.

Carol

How much did you say?

Expert 1

Four to five thousand pounds.

Carol

I feel faint, I can't believe it. Someone hold me up. *(The expert and six other men run over to hold Carol up. They all have their eyes on Carol's breasts)*

Mo

Janice, how did you get on?

Janice

He thought it was a fake.

Mo

He did, did he? Come with me. *(Mo and Janice go up to the Expert 2)* Excuse me. What's this I hear about you calling this object fake?

Expert 2

It feels not right to me, as though it is made of plastic.

Mo

The only plastic you will feel is your head when it's had plastic surgery. *(She holds up the club)* Now how much did he say it was worth, Janice?

Janice

Twenty to thirty pounds.

Mo

Did he? Would you like to revise your valuation?

Expert 2

(Shaking) I'm sure I said, two to three hundred pounds.

Mo

I knew you had got it wrong. *(Shouting to Sarah)* I think I've got your a new member for your club.

Sarah

Those little legs look as though they need stretching a bit *(to expert 2)* come with me NOW!

Expert 3
Now young lady what have you brought with you today?

The Fella Bella
A pair of Mary Quant's knickers.

Expert 3
Can we see them? *(The Fella Bella lifts up her dress to reveal the knickers. There are gasps from the audience)*

The Fella Bella
On the back it says "Virgins want to have fun".

Expert 3
And do they?

The Fella Bella
All the time.

Expert 3
Well I must admit, I've never valued anything in this way before. But you must have something worth two to three hundred pounds between your legs.

The Fella Bella
That's what I said to the last guy who took me out. He put a string of pearls around my lower bits. They were priced at four to five hundred pounds. *(As the Fella Bella walks away, the Expert and the audience are shown with their mouths open)*

Phoebe
Sarah love, you couldn't give him *(Expert 1)* a couple of turns on the rack, could you? He did nothing but stare at mine and Carol's breasts.

Sarah
Did he now? You leave it to me. *(She walks off)*

Mo
Well I didn't think I was going to enjoy it, but I've had a good day.. What about you girls?

Phoebe
I would certainly come again. What about you Janice?

Janice
Yes, I've loved it, but I think next time, I will bring the right club. This one I bought for one of my grandchildren a few years ago, so he could play Fred Flintstone in his school production.

Mo
So the expert was right?

Janice
I'm afraid so.

Mo
Well looking at his smiling face when he came off Sarah's rack, I think we did him a favour. *(They all laugh)*

Phoebe
I think it's time we got back.

Mo
Come on Carol, let's be having you. *(They walk past the rack)*

Sarah
Phoebe would you like to turn the wheel?

Phoebe
I'd love to *(screams are heard)*

Carol

What about you Carol?

Carol

Yes please. *(More screams can be heard)*

Dennis

Come on everyone. Let's have you back on the coach. *(They all get on. The coach sets off)*

Mo

How did you all get on?

Vera Viruse

Well he said my pill boxes were Victorian silver and worth one to two hundred each.

Mo

That's just the tonic you need. What about you Bella?

The Fella Bella

He said I have three hundred pounds between my legs.

Mo

And you a virgin. *(They all laugh)* What about you Sarah?

Sara

Well he said it was worth a hundred pounds, but each time I turned the wheel, it kept going up a hundred. It's now worth a thousand pounds. *(They all laugh)*

Mo

How much is that vase worth, Carol?

Carol

Four to five thousand pounds. I've decided to keep the vase and throw him in the bin. *(Laughter).*

Mo

Harold what about that ring?

Harold

He said it was worth one to two thousand.

Sarah

It's shit hot then? *(All laugh)*

Harold

Janice, what about your club?

Mo

Don't mention the club. She picked up the wrong one. That one, she bought for her grandchild, so he could play Fred Flintstone in the school production.

Harold

Janice, what are you like?

Mo

Well everyone, there is only one thing we can say to that!..

Everyone

Yabaddabadoo!

The Golden Girls

Characters

Sheila Ore

A small woman in her early nineties, very active, physically and sexually. She is the mother of Mickey the Policeman.

Taxi Driver

A young, good-looking man in his mid thirties.

Deb and Bev

Two women in their eighties. They dress like women in their twenties.

Jack

A gay man in his forties. He has a stocky build and works as a bouncer at the Laughing Cow.

Tony and Matt

A couple of young men in their twenties.

Setting

In the taxi
The Laughing Cow pub.

The Golden Girls

Mo is standing outside The Queen's Head, waiting for the taxi. Phoebe, Carol and Della Bella coming walking along

Mo

Here they come, the Golden Girls?

Phoebe

Hiya Mo. *(They all hug Mo)*

Mo

Bloody hell Phoebe love, how short is that skirt?

Phoebe

I'm single and ready to mingle.

Mo

You will be mingling with something by the end of the night, especially in that skirt. Carol, how tight is that top?

Carol

Well, I bought it as an extra large, but I forgot my pair are triple X large.

Mo

Well, all I can say is, be careful when you are dancing. You don't want to get two black eyes. *(They laugh)* As for you Bella, that outfit is so tight, you couldn't fit a hand in it.

The Fella Bella

That's the idea, it keeps those dirty pervs out of my knickers.

Mo

Have you got any on?

The Fella Bella

I forgot, I haven't got any on. *(They fall about laughing)*

Phoebe

I see you've gone for the married look. Flared trousers and a baggy top, right up to the neck.

Mo

I'm a woman with.

Phoebe

In that outfit you'd better get used to being a woman without. *(Laughing)*

Mo

Right, here comes the taxi. Bags the front

Phoebe

(In the taxi) Hello love *(to the taxi driver)* I've not seen you before.

Taxi man

No love, I've only been doing it a couple of days.

Phoebe

A bit of a virgin then?

Taxi man

Not much of a chance of that when I've got four beautiful women in my car.

Carol

I can see he's after a large tip.

Phoebe

I'll give him a tip. Always keep a woman on top

Mo

It's like a bloody 0898 number in here. I've not even had a drink yet.

The taxi pulls up at the traffic lights Another car pulls up beside them. Two young man are inside. Tony and Phoebe wind their windows down

Tony

(*To Phoebe*) Hi babe, how are you?

Phoebe

I'm very hot love. The heating is on full blast. It's because my friend in the front has a frozen heart.

Tony

I'm sure I could chip away at it. I'm Tony and this is my mate Matt.

Phoebe/Carol/Bella

Hi boys.

Tony

So what are your names then?

Phoebe

I'm Delilah, this is *(pointing to Bella)* Jane into pain. She's a dominatrix. This is me mate naughty Nora. She wears so many men out, they just can't keep up with her.

Tony

Bloody hell love, the size of them, I'm not surprised.

Phoebe

Her husband, Tony made them that large.

Tony

I bet he could get his whole body between them.

Phoebe

He does. The trouble is though, he gets lost in them for days. She had to call mountain rescue the other day. The rescue dog is still looking for him.

Tony

Did you know Delilah is my most favourite name in the whole world? *(Both the guys start to sing Tom Jones' Delilah. After three times they stop)*

Phoebe

You must be my Samson, because you can't see what twats you are making of yourselves. Bye.

Mo

Phoebe Dickson, you need a government health warning branding on you.

The Fella Bella

Well we are going to the Laughing Cow. *(They all start mooing)*

The taxi arrives outside The Laughing Cow. They get out and walk to the entrance

Carol

It looks like we are queuing. *(One of the bouncers calls out)*

Jack

Mrs Moore, *(they all turn round)* we can't have you queueing.

Mo

Hello Jack. It's wonderful to see you. Are you well?

Jack

Yes thanks, I'm very well.

Mo

I see you are back on the doors.

Jack

With the size of Sam, I need a job where I'm standing up.

Mo

Still together then?

Jack

Yeah. It's been over ten years now. Is it possible to have a chat with you later. I want to ask a favour.

Mo

Of course. Come and find me later. *(They all walk into the pub, where they see Sheila Ore at the bar with her two friends)*

Sheila Ore

Mo me little darling, how's it going?

Mo

Happy Birthday Sheila. Are you twenty-three today?

Sheila Ore

Twenty-two actually. If that young man over there keeps looking at me, I'll be feeling a twenty-two year old later. *(They laugh)*

Mo

Got you a little present.

Sheila Ore

Mo you shouldn't have done. *(She opens it)* Mo that's just what I needed. I'm down to my last condom and I've got a date next week.

Mo

You're welcome. You remember Phoebe?

Phoebe

Hi Sheila. Happy Birthday love.

Sheila Ore

Thanks. It's a good job she didn't get them from your shop. I would be pregnant after the first go, seeing that everything you sell is out-of-date.

Phoebe

I don't know what you mean.

Mo

You remember Carol?

Sheila Ore

How could I forget Carol. *(Looking at her breasts)* I can see you are still with your Tony. He's still handling you I see. You will have to put scaffolding up soon. *(Laughing)*.

Mo

This is Bella

The Fella Bella

Hi love.

Sheila Ore

You look amazing love. Have you had top and bottom done?

The Fella Bella
Just the top half.

Sheila Ore
They are getting two for one. You lucky girl.

Mo
Who's those two then?

Sheila Ore
These are me mates, Deb and Bev.

Mo
Hi girls. Are they both on the market?

Sheila Ore
They are on any market that is open. Buy one, get on free. *(They both laugh)* What are you drinking?

Mo
Sheila, I'm fine love.

Sheila Ore
I know you are. Barman, get my mate a double vodka coke.

Mo
I shall be on my back if I drink all that.

Sheila Ore
Believe me, on a Friday night, that's just where you need to be. *(Sheila walks away and starts dancing. Carol comes to the bar)*

Carol
Barman, double Malibu and coke please.

Mo

We have only been here five minutes. What number is that?

Carol

It's me third double. I've not paid for one yet.

Mo

Some things never change.

Carol

(To the barman) Can I have a double vodka coke as well?

Mo

That's not for you as well?

Carol

No, it's for you.

Mo

I know I'm going to end up on my back.

Carol

As long as it's you and not me. I'd never get up again. *(Laughing)* See you in a bit love.

The Fella Bella

(Coming to the bar) Barman can I have a double gin and tonic and half of cider?

Mo

You on the cider love?

The Fella Bella

You having a laugh. That's for him. He's driving.

Mo

I wonder where he'll be driving you later?

The Fella Bella

Paradise I hope. Nearly forgot, a double vodka coke.

Mo

Never mix your drinks love. You never know who might take advantage of your virginity.

The Fella Bella

It's a good job then, that I have bought it for you. See you later love.

Mo

Bloody hell, Ron's going to kill me.

Phoebe

How's it going Mo?

Mo

Phoebe, they keep buying me doubles.

Phoebe

That's shocking. You a mother with child.

Mo

Taking about children, who's that you are dancing with?

Phoebe

He's twenty-two and moves like John Travolta. That's just his hands. Do you know Mo, I can always relate to guys that age. In my mind I'm only a couple of years older.

Mo

See what you body says in the morning.

Phoebe
It will say I've been awoken at last.

Mo
Of course it will. I see you are still on the doubles.

Phoebe
Yes we are. *(She hands Mo a double vodka coke)*

Mo
Why can't I say no?

Phoebe
Because you are a drunken tart, like the rest of us.

After five minutes the music stops and the announcer comes onto the microphone

The Announcer
Ladies and gentlemen, just flown in from La Vegas.......

Sheila Ore
(Shouting) Piss off. Has he? He was round at eight this morning having a full English.

Man in crowd
Yeah, that full English was my boyfriend. I'm going to kill him.

The Announcer
.....The fabulous, the amazing, Isla Bligh. *(Everyone claps and cheers)*

Mickey
Good evening everyone. *(In full drag)* It's so nice to be here, where my roots are. Which is more than I can say with some of you lot. Have you never heard of a hairdressers before? It looks like you

have been in a snow storm. Now did I hear some one objecting to my full English? Well, when I cook a full English I always make sure I give them a full sausage. Not one of those cocktail ones, that you chew once and it's gone. I can see you are a muscle Mary.

Man in crowd

I'm at the gym every day

Mickey

You could be at the gym 24/7 love, but it's not going to make that maggot any bigger. Bouncer, throw Pee Wee out. No one wants a small dick man. My first song is for you all. *(He starts to sing I Am What I Am. At the end of the song everyone applauds)*

Phoebe

Great voice.

Mickey

Now everyone, there's a special lady in here tonight who is celebrating her birthday. Come onto the stage Mum. Where are you? *(Sheila staggers onto the stage)* Here she is the woman who gave birth to me.

Sheila Ore

He comes out with a fag in his mouth and a bottle of poppers up his nose.

Mickey

I can see someone's brought you some condoms for your birthday. You might leave mine alone now.

Sheila Ore

Don't bank on it. I've used two of them already.

Mickey

No wonder I never knew who my father was. Right everyone

after three. *(The whole pub sings Happy Birthday. As they do, a cake is wheeled out)* Mother enjoy your birthday. *(He gives her a big hug)*. This song is for you. *(He sings You Can Leave Your Hat On. As he is singing Jack the bouncer comes up to Mo)*

Jack

Is it possible to have a word now?

Mo

After three double vodkas, it's not the best time, but come on, let's find a quiet spot. *(They walk over to the back of the pub)* Now what can I do for you?

Jack

Well you know me and Sam have been together for a long time now.

Mo

How long has it been?

Jack

Well over ten years. Before you ask, I can enjoy it up me for over half an hour now.

Mo

That's better than ten minutes.

Jack

Anyway, it doesn't matter how hard we try, we are just not achieving fatherhood.

Mo

I knew I shouldn't have had that third double. So you are looking to adopt?

Jack

We are, but we need someone to give us a good reference.

Mo

Jack my reference won't be good it will be brilliant.

Jack

Mrs. Moore, I can see why they call you a saint.

Mo

You leave it with me. Now you had better walk me over to those drunken tarts. *(He walks Mo over and hugs her)*

Jack

Thank you.

Mo

You're welcome. *(He walks away)*

Phoebe

Mo get yourself up here. *(They are all dancing on the stage to Dancing Queen. Mo walks on the stage and starts dancing)*

Mo

Carol love, how can you dance with that young man's mouth clamped to your right breast?

Carol

My doctor said I was still capable of breast feeding.

Mo

But I don't think your Tony will be too happy when this young man is putting your milk on his cornflakes in the morning. Right girls, It's two o'clock and I'm off home. Ron is outside with the car.

Carol

Why. He's gone to the toilet. Let's slip out.

Phoebe

I'm ready. If someone can pick me up off the floor.

The Fella Bella

I'm definitely ready, since he's just bought me half a larger and lime. Do I look that cheap?

(They pick Phoebe up off the floor and stagger to the door)

Mo

I'll just say goodbye to Sheila.

Phoebe

I wouldn't bother, she's on her third condom in the end cubicle.

Carol

(Outside) There's your Ron. *(They all line up and start to sing Do Do Ron, Ron, Da Do Ron Ron)*

Mo

Right, now are we all in? We will drop off Bella first. Well, that was a good night.

Carol

Bloody great night. I didn't spend a penny.

Phoebe

You will after your first visit to the toilet. It will be flowing all night.

Mo

Here we are. Bella will you be alright?

The Fella Bella

Me? I might be pissed from the waist up, but these feet always get me home safely. Nite everyone.

Everyone

Night love. *(They wait till she opens the door and waves)*

Mo

Right Carol, you're next. So what happened to Sheila?

Phoebe

You mean what didn't happen to Sheila. I'm sure that end cubicle is her office. She had so many meetings in there tonight.

Carol

How old is she?

Phoebe

Ninety-three.

Phoebe/Carol

Lucky cow. *(They all laugh)*

Mo

Right Carol, this is you. *(Carol gets out of the door, trips and falls over the hedge, face down in Tony's dahlias)*

Phoebe

Not Tony's dahlias?

Mo

Shout up to him, so he can give her a hand.

Phoebe

(Shouting) Tony! Tony! *(Two minutes later Tony opens the bedroom window)*

Tony

What the bloody hell has she done? I'm coming down.

Mo

Come on Phoebe, let's get out of here before it all kicks off. *(They drive away)*

Phoebe

If only she had fallen into the daisies. But Tony's dahlias!.......

Mo

She won't be getting her cup of tea in bed for a bit. Right Phoebe love, this is you. *(She opens the door and falls out. Getting up she staggers up the path, showing her knickers).* I don't know how she's stayed single for so long. *(They both laugh)*

As Ron drives away, Mo cuddles up to him. Ron puts is arm around her

Mo

(Singing) I met him on a Monday and my heart stood still. Da do ron ron ron, da do ron ron.

A Quiet Day at the River-Not

Characters

Mo, Phoebe, Harold and Mary, Carol and Tony, Ron, Dick and Brenda, Billy, Tommy and Jenny.

Setting

Mo's home
By the river

A Quiet Day at the River-Not

Mo, Ron and Tommy are in the kitchen

Mo

Do you know, it's such a beautiful day, why don't we go and have a picnic down at the river?

Billy

That would be great Auntie Mo.

Mo

What do you think Ron?

Ron

Looking at Billy's face, I don't think I have much choice.

Mo

Well, it's ten o'clock now, so shall we say another hour. That will give me time to get some food ready.

Ron

Right I'll go and get the car out. *(Ron goes out)*

Mo

Billy, why don't you ever say Uncle Ron?

Billy

Because you're not married. Mother had many boyfriends in her life. But they were either not very nice, or were here today gone tomorrow.

Mo

Well we will have to see what we can do about that. Right what are you taking?

Billy

My phone and a football.

Mo

Forget about the phone. I want you to talk to the other people, not a machine.

Billy

Auntie Mo.

Mo

Don't you auntie Mo me. Go and get your football and your tennis rackets. *(He goes to his bedroom to find them)*

Ron

Are you ready?

Mo

I am. Go and put the food in the car. *(Ron takes the food)* Billy we are going.

Billy

I'm coming.

(They both walk out to the car)

Mo

Before you get into the car, young man, post your phone through the letter box.

Billy

I've left it in my bedroom.

Mo

Well its funny how it's found its way down your underpants then. Put it through the letter box.

Billy

Auntie Mo. *(Billy puts his phone through the letter box)*

Mo

Right I think we are ready. Off we go.

Billy

Dad let's me take my phone to bed.

Mo

Does he? I'll be having a word with him. Especially as school starts next week. Do you know Ron, to say it's bank holiday Monday, there's not many people around.

Ron

That's why I'm looking forward to a few hours of peace and quiet by the river.

(After half an hour driving, they reach the river)

Mo

Where should we park?

Ron

How about there? It looks quiet.

(After parking the car, they carry everything down to the river. They sit down on two deck chairs)

Mo

This is lovely, not a soul around.

Billy

Auntie Mo, what are those two ducks doing?

Harold

(Walking up) something in a distant memory. Hi everyone. Mary love put the picnic basket down here. We will give your auntie Mo a bit of company. Well girl I heard you were knocking back the vodka's the other night and you with child. Do you know Ron, she is lucky to have you, being the wayward woman she is.

Ron

I say that to myself everyday. *(They laugh).*

Harold

Did you hear that Bella was not a happy bunny?

Mo

No. What was up with her?

Harold

Well you know that ruff looking bloke that kept buying her drinks all night, because he tried to get in her knickers.

Mo

Yes.

Harold

Well apparently the gin he was buying was no Gordons. It was some cheap imitation stuff.

Mo

No.

Harold

What's more, she can't believe she got drunk on it.

Mo

Her street cred has gone right down.

Harold

That's just what she said.

Carol

(Walking over) Hi everyone. Fancy seeing you here. Tony put the food down here. I'll have my deck chair next to Mo in the shade. Hello Ron how are you my love?

Ron

Well thanks Carol. I didn't recognise you sober.

Carol

Don't Ron. As I was telling Tony, I only had a couple of lager and limes. I think it must have been the limes that were off. They affected my mental state.

Mo

Of course it was. *(Looking at Ron and Harold with their mouths open).*

Ron

How's your dahlias doing Ron?

Tony

I don't want to talk about it Ron. They were my pride and joy. *(He starts to cry)*

Carol

They were just a few flowers, you idiot. You need to man up. You don't need to grow dahlias you need to grow some balls.

Mo

Carol we are having a quiet afternoon.

Carol

Well I've got over the fact that he didn't bring me a cup of tea in bed, so he needs to get over that his dahlias are no-more.

Phoebe

Hi everyone. Have you missed me?

Mo

Of course we all have.

Phoebe

(Putting her bags of food down) Well I was going to have an hour on my own but seeing as you are all here. *(She puts her deck chair next to Mo).*

Mo

You didn't get the food from your place did you?

Phoebe

I was going to, but Mrs Tongue, you know the owner that looks like a lizard said I couldn't have any discount, due to the fact there was still a day left before they went out of date. So I went to Gino's deli. He always seems to undress you with his eyes.

Mo

That was not very long in your case, seeing as you don't wear much.

Phoebe

I don't know what you mean.

Mo

You must save tons of pounds each year, because you don't buy knickers and bras.

Phoebe

I don't need a bra as my breasts are still firm.

Mo

A firm favourite with any male that has a pulse.

Phoebe

You have become a bitter woman Mrs Moore. This time next year I will be known as Sister Mary Clare. I will be a nun.

Mo

Is that because you can be defrocked on a daily basis. *(They all laugh)*

Brenda

Hello everyone.

Mo

Hello you lot.

Brenda

Tommy what do you say to auntie Mo?

Tommy

Thank you auntie Mo, they are wicked trainers. *(He gives Mo a hug)*

Brenda

What about auntie Carol?

Tommy

Thank you auntie Carol for the packet of seeds.

Carol

You're welcome flower.

Brenda

He likes the colour of the dahlias the best. *(Tony starts crying again)*

Carol

Man up!

Brenda

Don't forget auntie Phoebe.

Tommy

Thank you auntie Phoebe for my money.

Phoebe

You are very welcome. Because your auntie Phoebe was on orange juice the other night, I could give you some extra pennies.

Tommy

But auntie Mo told mummy that you were that pissed you spent half the night on the floor.

Mo

It helps if they get to know you at an early age. *(They all laugh)*

Brenda

Don't forget to thank uncle Harold.

Harold

You're very welcome.

Brenda

Look, there's Mary and Billy over there playing football. Go and say hello the pair of you. Don't go near the river. *(They both run off)*

Mo
What was that? Orange juice?

Phoebe
Alright a couple of sherry.

Mo
You mean a couple of pints of sherry.

Everyone
I don't know what you mean. *(They all burst out laughing)*

Phoebe
Anyway was that Jack up my crack you were talking too?

Mo
It was. Do you know he is still with skinny Sam the ten inch man.

Phoebe
Would you believe it.

Brenda
Do I know these people?

Mo
I don't think you do.

Brenda
What's the story behind them?

Mo
Well,

Ron
Before you tell it, I'm off to play football with the kids, are you coming too?

Dick/Tony

Count us in. *(They get up and walk off towards the kids)*

Mo

As I was saying Skinny Sam the ten inch man, was always out every Saturday night at the gay club on Anal Street. He would always get off and take them back to his place. He would tell the guys he got off with that if they lasted for more than five minutes, then he would buy the drinks the following Saturday, but if they couldn't last the five minutes they would have to buy them.

Brenda

Who won?

Mo

Let's just say Sam took the same amount of money home with him that he had brought out.

Brenda

What about Jack up my crack?

Mo

Now there's a story. Well Jack up my crack was a bouncer at the arena. As you know they have many live acts on. Anyway, this pop group started to perform and Jack up my crack was on stage duty. He got the hots for the lead singer. Now, with thousands of young women screaming, Jack up my crack wasn't a happy bunny. Next minute a woman took her knickers off and threw them onto the stage. Jack up my crack went over to the woman and dragged her out. When he came back, he took off his own underpants and threw them on the stage. He was shouting your undies would look great on my bedroom floor. Next minute he started to climb onto the stage, showing his bottom to thousands of people. Now with loud boo's coming from the audience, the band changed their song to 'who let the dogs out' with the audience singing 'woof, woof, woof, woof' it took six bouncers to get him out.

Brenda

That's shocking. But how did he get a boyfriend like Jack?

Mo

Well you know how the other guys couldn't last for more than five minutes?

Brenda

Yes

Mo

Well Jack up my crack, lasted for over 5 minutes, hence the reason why they have been together for over ten years. The other night he told me he could last now for over half an hour. He told me that they had been trying for some time to have children, but haven't been successful. So he asked me if I would write them a reference.

Brenda

What did you say?

Mo

Well with three double vodkas in me. I said of course I will.

Brenda

You are wonderful *(everyone nods)*. Right lets get this food out. We have got enough here to feed an army.

Mo

While you do that , I'll walk over and tell them food is ready. *(As she walks over she sees Ron fouling Billy)*. That's a penalty!

Ron

You need to go to SpecSavers.

Mo

None of your lip young man. Give me the ball *(She puts the ball down on the penalty spot and takes the penalty)* Goal! *(She puts her arms up and runs around the field)*

Billy

Auntie Mo.

Mo

(She scoops Billy up and gives him a big hug) Right everyone, food is ready. *(They all walk over towards the food. Mo goes over to Mary)* I hear you are leaving us in a couple of weeks?

Mary

I am but I'm a bit scared auntie Mo.

Mo

Don't you be scared, my darling. You are going to have a wonderful time.

Mary

I hope so, but I don't know what I'm going to live on?

Mo

Well as you know the council has given you a grant to pay for your course and your accommodation.

Mary

Thank you so much for sorting that out for me.

Mo

You are very welcome. Now I know that uncle Harold has given you some money for your day to day living, but you can't live off baked beans every day. Now just before your mother died, she gave me ten thousand pounds for each of you. I was to give it to you when you needed it most. So what I'm going to do is set up an account in your name and put three thousand in for the first two years and four thousand for your last year. That way you will be able to but food and the books you need. Your mother had to go through a lot to save you this money. So spend it wisely.

Mary

(In tears) Thank you. *(She hugs Mo)*

Mo

Tonight when you look at the stars, send her a big kiss.

Mary

I will.

Mo

Come on young lady, let's go and eat. *(They walk over to the food)* I can see you have got your mouth full Phoebe Dickson. *(With her mouth full she puts her thumb up)*

After half an hour of eating. Brenda gets out the birthday cake and lights the candles. They all sing happy birthday to Tommy. Brenda cuts the cake

Brenda

Go round and give everyone a piece.

Carol

Do you know I fancy a game of tennis.

Phoebe

Do you really?

Carol

I do.

Phoebe

You will need some protective glasses.

Carol

Billy give me that racket. *(She takes the racket and walks towards the river)* Shouting scared of losing Dickson.

Phoebe

What did she say?

Billy

You are scared of losing auntie Phoebe.

Phoebe

Right I'll show her who's scared. Billy give me that other racket. *(She marches down the river)* Right best of three.

The first round Carol hits a high one and in trying to reach it Phoebe trips and falls back

Carol

First point to me.

Picking herself up, she hits the ball and Carol's breasts covers her eyes. The ball hits her on the head. Everyone laughs

Phoebe

Second point to me.

Carol

Right next point wins.

After hitting the ball a few times, Phoebe hits a high one. Carol trying to get it stumbles backwards and falls in the river

Mo

Oh my goodness!

Carol

Help!

Ron and Dick race down the bank to the river and manage to pull her out. Tony is laughing hysterically

Billy

That top auntie Carol's got on is a bit see through.

Mo

That's one way of putting it. Close your eyes.

Harold

You can see why Tony stays with her.

Carol

(To Tony) Look at the state of me I might of known you wouldn't save me.

Tony

You didn't save my dahlias. As I see it what goes around comes around.

Carol

Right get the deck chairs, we are going. *(Tony gets the deck chairs and they both walk towards the car. Tony can still be heard laughing)*

Mo

Well there's never a dull moment with those two.

Harold

Right come on Mary it's time we went. Mo I'll see you soon.

Mo

Mary work hard and enjoy yourself.

Mary

I will auntie Mo. *(She gives her a big hug)*

(As they both walk to the car Mary turns and waves to Mo)

Mo

Do you know, her mother did the exact same thing when I was walking off the market. I do hope she will be alright?

Brenda

With her mother inside her, she will be fine. Right Dick get everything together it won't be long before it's our twos bedtime. Children give your brother and auntie Mo a hug. *(They hug)* Next time you save someone from the river Dick please take off your socks and shoes first. Men!

After Brenda hugs Mo, they walk up to the car park

Mo

Well, so much for our quiet afternoon by the river.

Ron

I think if we found a river in Australia they would still find us.

Mo

Knowing that lot, they probably would. Shall we get some chips for supper?

Billy

Yes please.

Mo

Billy is that your phone ringing? *(He checks his pocket)*

Billy
Auntie Mo.

They are all seen hugging each other as they walk to the car

That's a Bargain

Characters

The Presenter

A young man in his early thirties. He is around six foot tall and has a friendly personality.

Phil

Small man in his mid sixties and he has been in the antique trade for over forty years. He's become arrogant.

Auctioneer

An average size man in his mid fifties.

Other characters

Mo, Phoebe, Harold.

Setting

Mo's home
In a courtesy car
In an auction house

That's a Bargain

Harold is banging at Mo's door

Mo

Bloody hell, who is it banging at my door at this time of the morning? *(She opens the door)* Harold are you alright?

Harold

(Letting himself in) Mo I've got a crisis.

Mo

You better come in, silly me, you are in. *(Mo goes through to the sitting room where Harold is already sitting on the sofa)* So what's up?

Harold

The BBC have just phoned me. They want to know if I can get two people to appear on 'That's a Bargain'. But the problem is they want two people, to be at the antiques fair in Bothingly, at eight tomorrow morning, to start filming.

Mo

Well I've got Carol coming in the afternoon, to make me a dress.

Harold

That's fine, you will be finished by one. Go on Mo, be a star.

Mo

What are you doing tomorrow?

Harold

I'm off to see Mary.

Mo
How is she getting on?

Harold
She is loving it. I think there might be a bit of love interest going on.

Mo
As long as it doesn't interfere with her studies.

Harold
So will you do it? Say yes.

Mo
Alright yes, I'll do it.

Harold
You are a star. But who else can we get at such short notice?

Mo
Bothingly is over fifty miles away.

Harold
Don't worry, the BBC are sending a car to your address.

Mo
What would of happened if I had said no?

Harold
You're a saint Mo, who can never say no and that's not just in the bedroom.

Mo
You are a naughty boy.

Harold

Spank me later. *(They both laugh)* So who can we ask? How about Carol?

Mo

No. She won't miss her cup of tea in bed.

Harold

What about Bella?

Mo

No. It takes her at least two hours to put on her slap.

Harold

Penny?

Mo

Her fingers won't look good on camera.

Harold

I know Sarah?

Mo

I don't think the rack could take that many people. What about Phoebe?

Harold

I thought she was working this weekend?

Mo

No. This weekend she's off.

Harold

Give her a ring *(Mo rings her. After five minutes, she answers the phone)*

Mo

Hello Phoebe love, can you be at mine for seven tomorrow morning? No I'm not taking the piss. BBC. See you tomorrow. *(She puts down the phone)*

Harold

Did she say yes?

Mo

Lets just say, if you mention the BBC, she will be crawling on all fours to get there.

Harold

Bless you Mo. Are you going to the switch on of the Christmas lights in a couple of weeks?

Mo

I'm sure I'll be there.

Harold

See you then love. *(They hug)*

The next morning, Phoebe is coming up Mo's path. She has a head scarf and dark glasses on. Mo opens the door.

Mo

Bloody hell, here she comes. 'Queen Cleopatra'

Phoebe

My mouth is that dry, I could drink the Nile. Get the kettle on girl.

After hugging, Phoebe goes into the living room. Mo comes from the kitchen with two cups of tea

Mo

You don't sound happy love?

Phoebe

We had the environmental health people in yesterday, which was a shock, seeing as they had to pass 'dirty Kath's café' to reach me.

Mo

What was the problem?

Phoebe

Someone complained that the packs of sausages were out of date. They said when they got them home and took them out of the packet, they were limp. I said, welcome to my world. They didn't see the funny side. I wouldn't mind so much, but they were only out of date by two days. By the afternoon I'm sitting there with the shelves empty.

Mo

Where was the owner?

Phoebe

Who, lizard features? She's on a cruise in the Med. Her third this year.

Mo

How the other half live. Come on love the car has just pulled up. They both get their coats on and walk to the car.

Phoebe

Morning driver. We are ready when you are.

Driver

Righty oh.

Phoebe
So what is it we're going to do?

Mo
They want us to be contestants on 'That's a Bargain'!

Phoebe
Never heard of it.

Mo
I think it's new.

Phoebe
As long as they don't start shooting until we've been in makeup.

Mo
This is going to be a long day then. They drive through one of the villages on the way to Bothingly.

Phoebe
Isn't that where 'Boozy Gill, that's always looked ill' used to live?

Mo
I think it is. Has she passed on?

Phoebe
Yes, many years ago.

Mo
How did she die?

Phoebe
You know how she was a heavy drinker?

Mo
Yes?

Phoebe

Well, back in the day, the brewery used to deliver all their beers and spirits by horse and cart each week to the surrounding villages. Well they always made a stop at Boozy Gill's place, due to the fact that she couldn't carry that many bottles from the offy anymore. No wonder she was bow legged. It was because of the weight of the bottles she has carried over the years. Anyway, she came out to collect her usual order, but as she did so, the horse tripped and a crate of vodka fell on Boozy Gills head. Well, the police came and said, to the doctor, "Is there any proof that is was the vodka that killed her?" The doctor said "Yes, a hundred percent proof." *(They both burst out laughing)* Mind you they always said the drink would kill her in the end.

Mo

Phoebe Dickson, what are you like? Looks like we are here. They get out of the car and walk over to the office. There is an assistant waiting for them.

Assistant

Good morning to you both. I hope you had a good journey?

Mo

Very nice thank you.

Assistant

Now what we are going to do is have a quick coffee. Then I will give you a quick rundown of how the show works.

Phoebe

Could you tell me at what time we get into makeup?

Assistant

There's not really much time for that.

Phoebe

Well I suggest you make time, looking at the bags under my eyes. I could save ten pence on a bag and carry my own shopping. Also looking at my friends' hair, she could play one of the 'witches of Eastwick'.

Assistant
I see what you mean.

Mo
I am here you know.

Phoebe
I'll tell you what we're going to do? We are going off to makeup now. You get the teas, one sugar and while they are making us look gorgeous, you fill us in with the format of the show. Right get with it. *(To the assistant)* Mo move yourself.

They both walk over to the makeup trailer, where the assistant brings them coffee and tells them how the show works

Mo
Phoebe, your face looks much better. You could only carry one bag instead of two.

Phoebe
Cheeky cow. We look gorgeous. Now let's go and make some gorgeous money.

They leave the makeup trailer and go to meet their expert

Assistant
Ladies, this is your expert Phil.

Phil
Morning ladies. Now I don't want you to be scared. I've been an expert for many years, so I will guide you through it all. Stick with

me girls. *(He winks at them)*

Phoebe

(Whispering to Mo) Where did he get this arrogant twat from?

They meet the other contestants with their expert. They are each given four hundred pounds and told they have an hour to get three items. They rush off to one of the tents, where there are fifty or so stands, with a variety of antiques on each table.

Phoebe

I like that. *(She picks us a glass vase)*

Mo

So do I, has it got a name on it?

Phoebe

It says 'Lalique'

Mo

They have got thirty on it.

Phil

There's no profit in that.

Mo

It's got 'Lalique' on the bottom.

Phil

Bound to be fake for that price. Let's go and look for something else.

Mo

Go and see, Phoebe, if you can get some money knocked off it. *(After two minutes Phoebe comes back)* Well?

Phoebe
I got it for ten pounds.

Mo
Well done you.

Phil
You will be lucky to make a profit.

They all walk further down the row. Mo spots a Moorcroft jug. She picks it up

Phoebe
I do like that.

Mo
I love the pattern on it. It looks rare to me.

Phil
Let the expert take a look. *(He inspects the jug)* No, it's not one of Moorcroft's best.

Mo
What date would you say?

Phil
Nineteen seventies. So it's not very old. With a ticket price of fifty pounds, you will be lucky to get twenty for it. I think its best we move on.

Phoebe
Go and ask Mo, what their best price is.

Phil
I'm telling you, you are wasting your time.

Mo

(Mo goes off and comes back two minutes later) He said he will do it for forty. So I brought it.

Phoebe

Well done you.

Phil

Well it's your funeral. Right we have twenty minutes left. I've seen a stall with some quality items on it.

They walk over to the stall. Phil picks up a piece of glass art

Phoebe

I do like that picture.

Phil

Never mind about that picture. This is the sort of thing you should be buying. It's a Victorian scent bottle. It has a silver top and not a bit of damage on it.

Mo

What's the ticket price?

Phil

A hundred and fifty pounds. That's a bargain.

Phoebe

Sounds a bit much to me. Let's just have a look at this picture. It's very beautiful. Could you just imagine Mo, living in that cottage and sitting in such a beautiful garden like that? It makes you want to go back to the Victorian times.

Mo

How much?

Phoebe
The ticket price is one hundred pounds.

Phil
You would be mad to pay that price.

Phoebe
I'll just see what I can get it for. *(She asks the store owner and comes back)* He said we can have it for eighty.

Phil
Forget that, it will make a loss, all day every day. Now this scent bottle, you will make at least fifty pounds on it. Are we all agreed it's the scent bottle?

Phoebe
Well we might have done. But I've brought the picture.

Phil
Well good luck to you. It's the last thing I would've brought.

Mo
That's our three items. Let's get back to the auction and see what profits we can make.

Phil
Don't you mean losses?

Later in the morning, they go to the auction house

Presenter
It's wonderful to see you both. Now how do you feel about your purchases?

Mo
Nervous. But I think we have made the right choices.

Presenter

Phil, with all your expertise, do you think they have made the right choice?

Phil

Let's just say they are not the three items I would have brought. I know each one is going to make a loss. But if you don't want to listen to someone who has been in the business for over forty years, then you get what you deserve.

Presenter

Well let's see who's right.

Auctioneer

A beautiful Lalique vase. Who's going to start me at a hundred? I've got five hundred on the internet. Five fifty, six hundred, six fifty. I've got seven hundred on the net *(pointing to a lady)* seven fifty, eight hundred on the net. Is there anyone else coming in? Last time, (the gavel comes down) sold for eight hundred pounds. *(Mo and Phoebe are seen hugging each other)*

Presenter

Well that was amazing. You made seven hundred and ninety pounds profit.

Phil

I can't believe it.

Presenter

Your next item is the Moorcroft jug. You brought it for thirty pounds.

Auctioneer

Can we start at a hundred pounds? I've got six hundred on the net. Six fifty, thank you miss, seven hundred on the net. Seven fifty in the room, nine hundred on the net. Nine fifty in the room, a thousand pounds on the net. Anybody else coming in? The last time at one thousand pounds. Sold for one thousand pounds. *(Mo and Phoebe are seen jumping up and down)*

Phoebe
I can't believe it.

Phil
Neither can I.

Phoebe
It seems it wasn't made in the nineteen seventies then. *(She looks at Phil)*

Presenter
You have made a profit of one thousand, seven hundred and sixty pounds. Here comes your last item, the picture brought for eighty pounds.

Auctioneer
What shall we say for this beautiful painting? Let's start at one hundred pounds. I've got a thousand pounds on the internet already.

Phoebe
Yes.

Auctioneer
One thousand one hundred, thank you sir. I've got one thousands three hundred on the net. One thousand four hundred anyone? Thank you madam. I've got two thousand on the internet.

Presenter
This is amazing, don't you think Phil?

Phil

I am in shock.

Auctioneer

Anyone else coming in? Sold at two thousand pounds. *(Both Mo and Phoebe are seen jumping for joy again)*

Presenter

You have now made five thousand six hundred and sixty pounds. Now you have Phil's bonus buy. What did you buy Phil?

Phil

I've brought that quality scent bottle.

Phoebe

Tell me you didn't pay a hundred and fifty pounds for it?

Phil

I did.

Mo

How much do you think it will make?

Phil

With such quality, it should double the price.

Presenter

Well ladies, what do you think?

Phoebe

He's been wrong on all our other items, so not a chance.

Presenter

So are you not going for it?

Mo/Phoebe
Never!

Presenter
Well we are going to sell it anyway. Here it comes.

Auctioneer
Fifty pounds anybody? No. Twenty pounds then? No. Let's start at a tenner, thank you. Fifteen, thank you. I've got twenty on the internet. Twenty five anyone? No, last call, sold at twenty pounds.

Presenter
Thank goodness you didn't go for it.

Phoebe
Thank goodness we didn't go with any of his suggestions. What was it? I've been an expert for forty years and with all my expertise I'm bound to be right. Well today we have seen your expertise. We all hope you find another hobby quickly. *(Phil, near to tears, walks off)*

Presenter
Well ladies, you have been amazing. You have made a profit of five thousand, six hundred and sixty pounds. You are our clear winners today. Well done.

Mo and Phoebe can be seen hugging each other, while everyone is applauding

That Time Again

Characters

Mayor

At all man in his mid-forties. He is single and very good looking.

Mini Meg

A small woman, in her mid-seventies. She was the Duke's cook for twenty years.

Other Characters

Mo, Phoebe, Janice, Bucket Bill, Billy, Harold, Mary, and Brenda and Dick with their two children, and Sweaty Betty.

Setting

The council house
The Christmas market

That Time Again

Mo
Hiya girls.

Phoebe/Janice
Hiya Mo. *(They all hug)*

Mo
Another year nearly gone. Where does the time go?

Phoebe
I know. Next year I will be heading towards my fifties.

Mo
Phoebe love, it's me you are talking to not your dating sites.

Phoebe
I've always said, 'you are as old as you feel'.

Mo
When was the last time you felt a man in his fifties?

Phoebe
Long time ago. The guys in their twenties and thirties get in the way.

Mo
Are you still talking to that guy inside? What was his name?

Phoebe
No. I've had to let him go, due to the fact someone smuggled a vibrator into him. *(She shows a picture of him using it)*

Mo

That smile of his face tells you a lot.

Phoebe

Exactly, seeing as he knows about my strap on, I don't think I would get much attention in the bedroom.

Mo

I'm sure you will get over it?

Phoebe

I already have, I've got a new friend in another prison.

Mo

What's this one called?

Phoebe

Psychotic Sam, the knife man.

Mo

Bloody hell Phoebe love, what's he inside for?

Phoebe

His ex-girlfriend didn't chop his veg up enough. So he showed her how to do it.

Mo

How many years did he get?

Phoebe

He got life. The judge said he had to do at least thirty years. I would love to cook him dinner.

Mo

Well he would be the man to cut you down to size. *(They both laugh)*

Janice

I hear there's a new Mayor this year.

Mo

After the last one, he couldn't be any worse.

Mayor

(Standing on the balcony of the council house) Welcome ladies and gentlemen, to the switch on of our Christmas lights.

Phoebe

He's a bit tasty.

Mo

Single as well. Make sure you cut his veg right, when you invite him for dinner. *(They all laugh)*

Mayor

This year the council have decided that a resident of the village should switch on the lights. We have chosen a woman who, not only has shown a remarkable determination to one family in particular, but has also given so much kindness to so many people in this village. Mrs Moore can you come up and join us .

Mo

I can't believe this.

Phoebe

Get yourself up there.

With a tear in her eye, Mo walks up the steps to the balcony

Mayor

Congratulations Mrs Moore.

Mo

Thank you. *(She turns to the audience)* I would like to thank you all for your applause. Also, I would just like to say I have lived in this village all my life and there is no other place I would rather live. Merry Christmas to you all. *(She switches on the lights)*

After five minutes Mo joins Phoebe and Janice

Phoebe

I don't know whether to curtsy or hug you?

Mo

A hug anytime.

Phoebe

What was the Mayor like, close up?

Mo

Very good looking.

Phoebe

I think I'll cook steak.

Mo

I think he bats for the other side. So he wouldn't cut the mustard. *(Laughing)*

They all walk over to Bucket Bill's stall.

Billy

Hello auntie Mo.

Mo

Hello Billy. Are you being a good boy?

Bucket Bill
He's being a wonderful boy. Such a great help.

Mo
Glad to hear it. Now can I have a pound of bananas and some grapes please.

Bucket Bill
Billy, can you serve this young lady?

Billy
What can I do for you Madam?

Mo
Your auntie Mo would like some bananas, so you can take one to school each day and some grapes. *(Billy puts the bananas and grapes into bags)*

Billy
That will be...

Bucket Bill
Free of charge.

Mo
Thank you Bill, it must be Christmas.

Bucket Bill
You are welcome.

Mo
Young man, you have school in the morning. I'll be back for you in a hour.

Bill
Auntie Mo

Mo

Don't you auntie Mo me, one hour.

All three of them walk away from the Bucket Bill stall

Phoebe

If I hadn't seen it with my own eyes, I wouldn't of believed it. How one man has changed so much.

Mo

That's what a nine year old boy has done to him. The love he has for his son has changed his world completely. I've heard he's even discovered his wife's body again. In fact he went to the dentist the other day. He even brought some deodorant from Boots.

Phoebe

The power of love.

Janice

Who's that walking over?

Mini Meg

Hello Miss Mo.

Mo

Hello Meg. How have you been?

Mini Meg

Yes I'm well.

Mo

How are you enjoying retirement?

Mini Meg

Very well. I wasn't looking forward to it, but with so many friends, I don't feel lonely at all. In fact I started up a cookery class two mornings a week. Even Penny pick a nose has joined. I do insist though that she scrubs her hands for half a hour each morning before she starts. I also make sure she puts a peg on her nose, so she can't get her fingers up there. Anyway, my bus is due. Merry Christmas Mo.

Mo

Merry Christmas Meg. *(She walks off)*

Janice

Where do you know her from?

Mo

She was His Grace's cook for many years. Although it was a bit touch and go at the start.

Janice

Why was that?

Mo

Well, when she got the job as the cook, His Grace thought as a nice treat he would buy her a new kitchen. So when they fitted all the units, they realised that Meg was only just over four foot high, hence the name Mini Meg. All the units were too high. So she couldn't reach the work surfaces to make the food.

Janice

So what did they do?

Mo

Well seeing as His Grace spent thousands on the kitchen, he brought her one of those small trampolines. So when she was making a cake she would jump whisk, jump whisk, it took forever. So his grace brought her some stilts. That did the trick. It developed her balancing skills beautifully. She used to perform at the circus on her day off.

Janice
That's amazing.

Phoebe
I couldn't believe they have got him back again.

Janice
Who?

Phoebe
'Dirty Bert up your skirt'

Mo
By the looks of his feet he's already had a few customers already.

Phoebe
His cheeks are as red as his costume. I see the carol singers are back again.

Sweaty Betty
(Shouting) Hi Mo.

Mo
Hi Betty love, I see you are still out then?

Sweaty Betty
Yeah I got out two weeks ago. I did a six month stretch.

Mo
(Shouting) Was it for ball tampering?

Sweaty Betty
Yeah, he couldn't get it up so I gave it a good kicking to see if I could kick start it up.

Mo

No movement.

Sweaty Betty

No. It was as limp as those out of date sausages Phoebe sells.

Phoebe

I don't know what you mean.

Mo

So you are back on tag then?

Sweaty Betty

I'm afraid so. I've put some Christmas lights around my ankle so it makes it look more festive. Merry Christmas Mo.

Mo

Merry Christmas Betty.

As they walk on, one of the stalls owner comes up to Mo with a big box of chocolates

First stall owner

Thank you for the wonderful thing you did.

Mo

Thank you very much.

Second stall owner

Thank you Mrs Moore. *(She gives her a big bunch of flowers)*

Mo

Thank you so much.

Third stall owner

We have clubbed together and brought you a gold cross to say thank you for what you did for one of our own.

Mo

(With tears in her eyes) Thank you so much.

They head towards Vee's stall, where there is a picture of her hanging up

Phoebe

It was such a shame for one to die so young and to leave four beautiful children.

Mo

Life has a funny way of working out for some.

As they stand there looking at Vee's picture, a crowd of people move together. Harold and Mary stand next to Mo, as does Brenda and Dick with their children. The choir walks over with all of the stall owners. With Billy holding Mo's hand, the choir starts to sing Silent Night. Everybody sings

The Christmas Blow and Go

Characters

Able Mable

A small woman in her eighties. She is a fortune teller who is as deaf as a post.

Other Characters

Mo, Phoebe, Janice, Vera Virus and Frigging Freda.

Setting

Blow and Go (the hairdressers)

The Christmas Blow and Go

Mo walks into the hairdressers and is confronted with fairy lights, tinsel and Christmas music

Mo
Morning everyone.

Everyone
Morning Mo.

Mo
It's like Santa's grotto in here.

Vera Virus
Bell got a bit carried away.

Mo
Well it's certainly camp as Christmas.

Vera Virus
I heard you were treated like a celebrity at the Christmas market.

Mo
I don't know about a celebrity, but they all certainly looked after me. I've never had so many flowers and chocolates given me.

Vera Virus
It reminds you of the flower people in the nineteen sixties. Loads of sex and drugs.

Mo
Of course. I was too young to remember the sixties.

Vera Virus

Piss off. They used to call you Marijuana Mo gives the best blow *(everyone starts to laugh)*

Mo

How dare you. I kept my virginity until marriage.

Vera Virus

Of course you did. *(Everyone falls about laughing)*

Mo

I'm a saint not a sinner *(she sticks two fingers up)* who's that in the corner?

Vera Virus

I thought I would invite Mable to tell a few fortunes.

Phoebe

That's who it is, Able Mable.

Janice

How did she get that name?

Phoebe

Let's just say she was always able to get things wrong. There was a time a young woman who was getting married went to see her. She said the cards told her that the man she was to marry would be unlucky and never achieve anything. So she broke off the engagement. Two months later, at the day they were supposed to get married, he won millions on the lottery, married and now has four children.

Janice

What happened to her?

Phoebe

She went mad and was committed to an asylum.

Mo

Then there was that young guy who went to see her, she told him the cards were telling her that he would marry a beautiful young woman and they would be in love with each other, for the rest of their lives. Two months later, he came out as gay. What was his name?

Phoebe

Rob, sucks nob.

Mo

That was him.

Phoebe

Don't forget that woman, who was told she was going to win a fortune.

Janice

She didn't.

Phoebe

She did. So the woman went out and brought a car. Booked various holidays and was a frequent visitor to all the designer shops.

Janice

What happened to her?

Mo

She never won a penny. She was found two weeks later swinging from a tree. They told Mable what had happened.

Janice

What did she say?

Mo

Well at least it was a designer scarf she killed herself with.

Janice

That's terrible. I hope she didn't hear what we have been talking about?

Mo

No. She is as deaf as a post.

Vera Virus

Why don't you have your cards read? She has already read ours.

Mo

Don't tell me you are all going to end up with rich husbands.

Vera Virus

You must of been that fly on the wall. She said Janice was going to slim down, which would enable her to get whisked off her feet.

Mo

Really?

Vera Virus

Well only a crane could pick her up at the moment.

Janice

Do you mind.

Vera Virus

She said, Phoebe will be cooking a five course meal. With the course being a thick piece of beef.

Mo

Now why does that not surprise me.

Vera Virus

She said I was going to get a string of hairdressers and make cushions stuffed with human hair.

Mo

I hope you told her to get stuffed?

Vera Virus

I did, but as you know she is as deaf as a post. Anyway get yourself over there. *(Shouting)* Mable, I've got you another customer.

Able Mable

Hello young lady.

Phoebe

Looks like she is taking the piss already.

Able Mable

I want you to take a card from the top and then from the bottom *(Mo does this and places them on the table)* Death. *(She starts screaming and banging the table)* it's alright it's someone else's death.

Mo

She needs putting down.

Able Mable

(She looks at the second card) Where death was seen at the start of the year, now life will be seen at the end of the year. Something beautiful is coming. *(She puts her hand out for the payment. Mo gives her some money. Then walks back)*

Mo

I know it's Christmas, but that was taking the piss.

Frigging Freda comes in

Frigging Freda

Morning ladies.

Everyone
Morning Freda.

Frigging Freda
I see you have got Able Mable here. Hello Mable. *(Mable takes one look at Freda and starts screaming. She rushes out of the hairdressers shouting 'ghost')*

Mo
That's one way of getting rid of her. What's that ghost thing all about?

Frigging Freda
She read the cards last year for me. She said, death was on its way for me.

Phoebe
Did death come?

Frigging Freda
No. I'm still here love.

Phoebe
So you are a ghost? That's funny you have frightened the life out of me for years.

Mo
Able Mable must have meant your love life. That's been dead for years.

Frigging Freda
I'm just very picky.

Mo
So are the blokes. *(Everyone laughs)*

Frigging Freda
Did Vera tell you about Stella?

Mo
No.

Frigging Freda
She has handed her notice in.

Mo
Is that right Vera?

Vera Virus
She has. She told me she is going into modelling. She has already got several jobs after Christmas. She is coming next week to the ball. I hear the Duke is not very well?

Mo
By the sounds of it, he will be lucky to last out the year.

Phoebe
It's a shame. But we can't live forever.

Mo
I have a feeling this could well be the last Christmas Ball at the Manor. I'm sure that greedy, nasty son of his wouldn't want to bother with us peasants.

Phoebe
Well we will have to make it a good one.

Mo
So what is everyone up to this Christmas? What about you Janice? Are you spending it with your daughter?

Janice

Well I was going round on Christmas day, but she phoned me and we had to cancel Christmas.

Mo

Nothing serious I hope.

Janice

Well you know how they are trying for a baby?

Mo

Yes.

Janice

Well she's found out that the Christmas period is the time she is at her most fertile. So she said to me, it wouldn't be right to be laying the table for Christmas dinner one minute, then lying on it with her legs apart the next minute. I wouldn't be able to look at a turkeys leg in the same way ever again.

Mo

See what you mean. What about you Phoebe love?

Phoebe

You know me love. Christmas day has always been an open house day. It gives me the chance to cook for more than one.

Mo

If it was anything like last year, you will be cooking for a hundred and one.

Phoebe

Well, no-one should be alone on Christmas day. What about you?

Mo

It was going to be the three of us. But Harold was on the phone the other day, inviting us around to his place. He thought as it was the first Christmas without Vee, the children should be together.

Phoebe

He has got a point.

Mo

That's what I thought. So he's cooking for nine this year. By the sounds of it he can't wait.

Frigging Freda

I met her once you know.

Mo

Who?

Frigging Freda

The Queen.

Mo

Did you?

Frigging Freda

I did. It was a race meeting.

Mo

Did you speak to her?

Frigging Freda

No. Although I was only a few feet away from her. The horse I backed won half a length in front of her horse. I'm sure she saw me jumping up and down then it won. Five minutes later, she walked past me. I was doing my curtsy when I got cramp in my leg and fell over. The hand with the winning ticket in, was sticking out. When she walked by she trod on my hand.

Mo
She didn't?

Frigging Freda
She did. I'm sure I heard her say "It's about time they put that old hag down!"

Mo
Well, the Queen always was a good judge of character. *(They all laugh)*

Vera Virus
You will never guess who I saw the other day?

Mo
Who?

Vera Virus
Carol Corpes.

Mo
Is she still with us?

Vera Virus
Just. She looks like a dead woman walking.

Janice
How did she get that name?

Vera Virus
It's a bit of a sad story really. She married a bloke called Richard Head and before you say it, he was a dick head, but not in the way that you are thinking.

Janice
In what way then?

Vera Virus

He was gay. In fact, he was as gay as Christmas.

Janice

That gay.

Vera Virus

That gay. Mind you, there was many a guy in those days who got married to cover up their sexuality. Anyway she loved it round the back, so the sex was fine. After a few years though, her front bottom felt a bit neglected. So they started to invite men round for three somes. He would take them from the back and she would have them round the front. However, after a night out at 'Arthurs or Martha's' night club, they brought back a dwarf. Now this was alright for Richard, but left Carol frustrated. She looked at his bits and said "I've cooked bigger carrots than that" Well the dwarf went mental. He ran into the kitchen to get a knife. Luckily the knives were in the top draw. But they did watch him, jumping up and down, trying to get them. After five minutes he ran back into the living room and just before he was about to punch Carol in her front bottom, Richard got between them and got the full force of his semi-penis.

Janice

No.

Vera Virus

He fell down in agony, had a heart attack and died. The dwarf escaped through the cat flap. It took the police two days on bended knees to find him. At court the judge said to the dwarf "I bet this is this is the only time in your life when your size did matter. Well the courtroom erupted into laughter, which was continues when the dwarf said he was aiming for the face. For the next twenty years Carol went into a deep mourning. A bit like Queen Victoria did.

Janice

That's terrible.

Vera Virus

Last year it would of been their fiftieth wedding anniversary. So Carol got it into her head that she wanted to renew their wedding vows. She booked the church, reception and sent out invitations. The day came and wearing a beautiful outfit from 'Marks' she walked down the aisle to where Richard's coffin was standing up right at the front.

Janice

Tell me they didn't dig him up?

Vera Virus

No. The undertakers borrowed a skeleton from the university and dressed it up in Richards clothes. They put him into one of their empty coffins. The vicar who was 'pissed up Pete, who liked it neat' conducted the service. Every time Richard had to speak in the service, the undertakers knocked on the back of the coffin to say yes. When 'pissed up Pete who liked it neat' had finished talking, the undertakers opened up the coffin, so that Carol could give him a kiss.

Janice

She didn't?

Vera Virus

She did. What's more, the undertakers wheeled the open coffin up the aisle with Carol holding the skeletons hand. It's not everyday you see your guests open mouthed or collapsing on the floor. They travelled to the reception in a hearse, with Carol lying down, next to the coffin. At the reception, Carol wanted to have the first dance with her Richard. So the undertakers attached metal rods to the skeleton to keep it up right. They danced with the skeleton as it had its arms around Carol.

Janice

What was the song they danced to?

Vera Virus
'Hello' By Lionel Richie.

Janice
What did the guests think?

Vera Virus
It was a free bar.

Janice
Could it get any worse?

Vera Virus
It could. At eleven o'clock, Carol, who had booked a room for the night, was seen walking up the stairs, carrying the skeleton in her arms.

Janice
She didn't?

Vera Virus
Nobody knows. But the next day, when the undertaker took the skeleton back to the university, the university wasn't happy.

Janice
Why?

Vera Virus
All the fingers were missing off the skeletons right hand.

Janice
Stop it now.

Vera Virus
That's why they call her the five fingered widow.

Janice

It cuts you to the bone. *(They all burst out laughing)*

Frigging Freda

I say Phoebe do you think you will have Sarah Summers again this year?

Phoebe

It all depends if she wants Santa to come down her chimney with a full sack.

Janice

What was that all about?

Phoebe

Well, as a little girl, she had always dreamed of Santa coming down her chimney. So last year, she told 'Ben Hung' to put on a Santa outfit with one alteration.

Janice

What was that?

Phoebe

He had to put on a small, tight pair of red lycra shorts. A bit like what Kyle wore when she was dancing with Justin Timberland. She said, it was so hard to cram it all in. Anyway, she said, "Right get yourself on that roof and down the chimney.

I want to see my stockings full by the morning." She did say he looked worried, on account he hated heights. But when she cracked the whip, he wiped his tears away and got climbing. An hour later she was woken up by someone banging on her door. It was the fireman. A neighbour had phoned them saying they had seen Santa falling down the chimney, she said "they all rushed to the living room" When the got there, the fireman looked up, and saw Santa trapped half way down.

Santa said "Ho ho ho mistress, have I got a surprise for you." The trouble was though his lycra shorts had split, so it was the fireman who got the full surprise seeing all Santa's bits dangling. Santa had broken two legs and a concussion, but as Sarah said it could have been worse, it could have been three broken legs. *(They all burst out laughing)*

Mo

Right I must get on.

Vera Virus

Before you go, I hear Carol has made you a beautiful white dress, for the ball.

Mo

Is nothing secret around here?

Vera Virus

Well you know I'm going to that wedding after new year.

Mo

Yes.

Vera Virus

Well I've bought myself a beautiful flowered brooch. It will look wonderful on your dress. So I'm going to lend it to you.

Mo

You don't have to do that?

Vera Virus

Yes I do. I'll pop it round at the weekend.

Mo

That's so kind Vera *(she gives her a hug)* see you all at the ball.

Everyone
Bye Mo.

Mo
Bye everyone.

She opens the door and walks up the street.

A Special Christmas

Characters

All the characters that have featured throughout the different chapters.

Settings

Mo's home
The Manor House

A Special Christmas

Mo is making mince pies in her kitchen. She hears a knock on the door. Opening the door, she sees it's the Duke

Mo

Good morning Your Grace, what a nice surprise.

The Duke

Good morning to you.

Mo

Do come in. *(The Duke comes in and goes to sit in the living room)*

Mo

Can I get you anything?

The Duke

Just a little of your time would be nice.

Mo

Yes of course. *(She sits down)*

The Duke

What a lovely tree. It's beautifully decorated.

Mo

Thank you. With a young one living here now, I thought I would make a special effort.

The Duke

How's that working out for you?

Mo

Very well Your Grace. He is such an enduring child, you can't help but love him. Especially knowing where he has come from and all the things he must have seen and heard in his young life.

The Duke

How are you getting on with your boyfriend?

Mo

Who Ron? Do you know Your Grace, I never thought I would find love again, after us. But someone must be smiling on me from above.

The Duke

The Lord always smiles on the righteous. Believe me. There is not another woman who is more deserving. As I have told you many times, I loved you so much then as I do now, I should have left everything behind, to be with the woman I loved. But I chose not to and because of it, I became only half the man, who never experienced love again with any other women. In fact, the only love I have left was for our son, because he was a part of you.

Mo

How is he Your Grace?

The Duke

He's spending my last Christmas with me. I must get him to pop over and visit you.

Mo

That would be nice.

The Duke

Now before I go, I want to give you a Christmas present. In fact, I want to give you two.

Mo

Your Grace, there is no need.

The Duke

There is every need. Now this is your first one. *(He hands Mo an envelope)* Do open it. *(She opens it)*

Mo

Your Grace, thank you so much.

The Duke

I wanted to make sure that you always have a roof over your head. As my time is short. I didn't want my successor to have the power to evict you. So now with the deeds to the property, you and your family are secure.

Mo

Thank you Your Grace.

The Duke

Your second present is something I brought for you, over thirty years ago. But circumstances as they were, I never had the chance to give it to you. *(Mo opens the present, to be confronted by a diamond and emerald engagement ring)*

Mo

Your grace, this is beautiful. Thank you so much. *(She hugs the Duke)*. You will always be in my heart.

The Duke

You are very welcome. Now its time for me to go.

Mo

I'll see you out Your Grace. *(As they reached the door, Ron and Billy are coming up the path)*

Ron

It's so nice to see you, Your Grace.

Mo

This is Billy Your Grace.

Billy

Hello mate. Is that your car Mr?

The Duke

It is.

Mo

Billy, this is His Grace, The Duke of Cavendish.

Billy

Do you live in that big house?

The Duke

I do.

Billy

You must be loaded mate.

Mo

Billy, close your lips.

The Duke

Never forget sunshine, all the money in the world, will never buy you love. Goodbye Mrs Moore. *(As Ron and Billy go indoors, Mo is seen waving from her front step)*

At around eight o'clock in the evening, Mo leaves her home and can be seen walking along the lane to the manor. As she reaches the gate and walks up the long drive way, she can see Phoebe and Janice waving to her in front of the manor house. As she reaches them, she gives them both a big hug

Mo

Merry Christmas to you both.

Phoebe/Janice

Merry Christmas Mo.

Mo

Well, here we are again. Where does the time go?

Phoebe

I know. It doesn't seem five minutes since we were here last year. Its certainly been a year we will never forget.

Mo

We certainly won't.

Phoebe

There was the tragic death of Vee, with new lives for her children.

Janice

How is your Billy?

Mo

I had His Grace come round this morning and Billy kept addressing him as 'mate' and 'Mr'. But do you know ladies, he will always be a person who stays true to himself throughout his life and for that you have to love him.

Phoebe

Then your son came back into your life.

Mo

That was a blessing. To know I had become a grandmother at such a young age.

Phoebe

Maths was never your best subject was it?

Mo/Janice

I don't know what you mean. *(They all laugh)*

Phoebe

Don't forget about the game shows.

Mo

They were a bit outrageous.

Phoebe

I heard that twat of an expert got the sack. In fact, they are not sure whether they are going to make anymore.

Mo

Lets face it, you can't improve on perfection.

Phoebe

Too right.

Janice

Don't forget Brenda's wedding.

Mo

That was a nice day.

Phoebe

I've heard ever since they went to the 'Palace of Versailles and saw the hall of mirrors, Dick has got a bit carried away. He has put mirrors up on their bedroom ceiling. Brenda said she doesn't mind, but, now she has to go to the hairdressers once a week to get her roots done. Right madam. Let's have a look at this dress that Carol has made you. *(Mo opens up her coat)* That looks wonderful Mo.

Janice

It's beautiful. That flowered broach that Vera lent you looks amazing.

Phoebe

That cross and chain sets the whole outfit off beautifully. Is that new?

Mo

Yes. It's what the market traders bought me.

Phoebe

It looks wonderful.

Janice

Who's this coming up the drive?

Mo

It's Bertha and Lil. Merry Christmas ladies.

Bertha

Merry Christmas Mo.

Mo

Are you still going to 'Fat Free World'?

Lil

No. Didn't you hear, that vile Kevin got the sack.

Mo

Why?

Lil

They found out that he had fixed the scales. So every time we were weighed, the scales said we were heavier than we were. We found out that we were five stone lighter than we thought we were.

Mo

What happened to him?

Lil

Last heard he was washing dishes in a Chinese restaurant. Every time the staff bring him the dishes to wash, they bow and say 'ass hole!' *(They all burst out laughing)*

Bertha

See you all later

Mo

What goes around comes around.

Phoebe

The police are here.

Policeman Mickey

Merry Christmas ladies. *(He hugs everyone)*

Sheila Ore

Merry Christmas Mo *(hugging)* I wouldn't miss this night for anything.

Policeman Mickey

We can't stay too long. Mother's got a couple of blokes lined up in the end cubicle of the Laughing Cow you know what it's like after going without it for a couple of days.

Sheila Ore

It's bloody frustrating. You look as though you have lost some weight Mo. You are definitely not going without. They say it's equal to a five mile jog. I bet you are doing twenty miles a night. See you later love. Come on Mickey, lets see if we can find you a bit of trade.

Janice

Isn't that the receptionist at the hospital?

Shirley

Hello ladies.

Mo

Merry Christmas Shirley love.

Shirley

Last week Mo, you would have laughed.

Mo

Why?

Shirley

Well a young man came in, apparently he was a roofer. Anyway, I asked him his name and address, but all he could do was shake his head and point to his mouth. Well, I asked him several times. In the end I said "Look here twat face, stop taking the piss. I said I haven't got the time to mess about with idiots like you." Anyway, a nurse came to collect him. I said to her "The twat wouldn't tell me his name." She said "He wouldn't do as he has got a nail through his tongue."

Mo

No?

Shirley

Apparently he was using one of these nail guns when he tripped and put a nail through his tongue. I felt so bad, you could have nailed me to a cross. I was crucified. See you all later.

Jack

(Jack walks straight up to Mo and hugs her) Thank you so much. Myself and Sam will never forget what you did for us.

Sam
We are going to collect our little boy in a couple of weeks. Thank you. (*He gives Mo a hug)*

Mo
You will both make wonderful parents. Merry Christmas to you both. *(They both walk off to the manor)*

Next to come along are the market traders. They take it in turns to shake Mo's hand and to wish her a Merry Christmas. After the market traders, the choir can be heard coming up the drive, singing jingle bells. They all wave to Mo. Sweaty Betty walks over to Mo, giving her a big hug.

Mo
Merry Christmas Betty. 'Jingle Bells' is one of my favourites.

Sweaty Betty
I've put some bells around my tag.

Mo
Very festive love.

Sweaty Betty
That's just what I thought. See you later flower.

Phoebe
Here comes the ladies of the night, with dirty Kath.

Mo
Merry Christmas to you all. *(They all hug Mo in turn)*

Janice
Here comes mini Meg and Penny pick a nose.

Mo

Merry Christmas to you both.

Mini Meg

A Merry Christmas to you too. Go on Penny, tell Mrs Moore what you have made this Christmas.

Penny

I made a Christmas Cake and there wasn't a piece of green on it.

Mini Meg

Why was that?

Penny

Because I always scrub my hands before I start. I even get right under my nails. I feel like a new woman.

Mo

Well done to you. That will give everyone a Christmas present this year. *(They walk off)*

Phoebe

Here comes Lassie and her bitch.

Mo

Phoebe Dickson, wash your mouth out with some out of date soap. Merry Christmas ladies.

Donna

Merry Christmas Mo.

Mo

Gemma, how are you?

Gemma

Much better thanks. In fact I've had no pain ever since they were taken out. Although I do miss one thing.

Mo
What's that?

Gemma
Donna's fingers creaming my bottom. We will see you later.

Phoebe
Dirty bitch.

Mo
Hello Gill. Merry Christmas.

Pill Gill
Merry Christmas to you all.

Mo
That's a big smile Gill

Pill Gill
I've got myself a boyfriend.

Mo
Have you?

Pill Gill
I have, but I'm not supposed to tell anyone. His name is Peter, he is spiderman.

Mo
Is he?

Pill Gill
He is. I leave my bedroom window open over night. With his spider webs, he flies through it. Although sometimes, if he flies

too quick, he smacks his head on my bedroom wall. That's alright though, because, I just change my costume from Wonder Woman to Florence Nightingale. I've got rid of the cobweb on my front bottom to a spider web.

Phoebe
I think a trip to the asylum wouldn't go a miss, for that one.

Mo
Here they all come, the blow and go girls.

Vera Virus
Merry Christmas to you all. Show us your dress. *(Mo undoes her coat)* You look amazing. Bella, what do you think?

The Fella Bella
You look wonderful. That brooch is perfect.

Mo
Thank you, Who's this with you?

Stella
Hello Mrs Moore.

Mo
It can't be. You look so beautiful.

Janice
Who is it?

Mo
It's Stella.

Janice
Never. So beautiful.

Mo

Come and give me a hug. *(She does)*

Frigging Freda

Right girls, let's get in. I can feel the snow coming. *(They all walk off)*

Mo

Do you know, there seems to be far more people here than last year.

Phoebe

It's probably because it's the last one.

Janice

Merry Christmas Dennis.

Dennis

A Merry Christmas to you ladies. *(He comes up to Mo and kisses her on her cheek)*

Mo

Merry Christmas Dennis. *(He walks off)* Well that's never happened before.

Phoebe

You're right, it's never happened in public. But in private, that's another matter. *(They all laugh)*

Mo

Here they both come. I wonder what Tony has done wrong this Christmas.

Carol

Merry Christmas ladies.

Mo
Merry Christmas Carol.

Carol
Do you know that husband of mine?

Mo
Yes?

Carol
Well he's not done a thing wrong,

Mo
You could knock me down with a feather.

Carol
I know, it's pissing me right off. Before I forget, look what I brought from the market today. *(She lifts up her dress to reveal a blue garter at the top of her leg)*

Mo
That looks nice Carol.

Carol
I'm glad you think so. I've brought one for you.

Mo
Thank you Carol.

Carol
Right girls gather round. Lets get it on.

Mo
You can't put it on now?

Carol

Of course we can. No-one's looking. Besides, you know what men are like after a couple of drinks. Here you are Phoebe *(passing her the garter)* Get it on. If I go too low I'll topple over with this pair *(Phoebe puts the garter onto Mo's leg)* The colour blue always did look good on you. Right come on you, lets get in.

Phoebe

Don't look now, but here comes Tina.

Tina

Merry Christmas ladies.

Phoebe

Merry Christmas Tina, I see you have a friend with you?

Tina

This is young Guy 'who keeps it up all night'.

Phoebe

Very nice,

Tina

Mo, I want to give you something of our Mother's. *(Mo takes the box and opens it)*

Mo

It's beautiful.

Tina

It is old, but it is still very wearable. Do put it on. *(Mo puts it on and smiles)*

Mo

Thank you Tina. *(They both hug, Tina and Guy walk off)*

Janice
Well you don't see that every day.

Phoebe
Talking of old boys. Here comes Sarah and Ben. Merry Christmas Sarah.

Sarah
Merry Christmas to you all.

Phoebe
Will I see you tomorrow?

Sarah
I shouldn't think so. I've decided to let Santa come through the window this year. I don't want the same fiasco as last year.

Ben
I'm so sorry mistress.

Sarah
You will be if I don't get my stocking filled this Christmas. *(They walk off)*

Mo
Merry Christmas Harold. Merry Christmas Mary.

Harold
Merry Christmas ladies. One o'clock alright Mo?

Mo
That will be fine. Everything alright with you Mary?

Mary
Yes thank you auntie Mo.

Mo
Working hard I hope?

Mary
It's hard work, but I do love it.

Mo
Well done you.

Harold
See you all later.

Mo
That must be about it?

Phoebe
Who's this coming?

Brenda
Merry Christmas to you all.

Mo
Merry Christmas.

Tommy/Jenny
Merry Christmas auntie Mo. *(They both hug her)*

Mo
It's a bit late for you two to still be up?

Brenda
I thought as it will be the last one, it will be nice for them to come. It's certainly getting colder. We'll see you in a bit.

Mo
Right have we done?

Janice

Not quite

Mo

Well there's nobody else left.

Billy

(Shouting from a distance) Merry Christmas auntie Mo.

Mo

What is going on? *(Bill and his wife walk up the drive with Billy. Billy runs ahead and gives Mo a big hug)* What are you all doing here?

Bucket Bill

Billy wanted to come and see his mate the Duke, as it's Christmas. *(Bill goes and hugs Mo)* See you all later.

Mo

Am I missing something?

Phoebe

Yes, your grandchildren, coming up the drive.

James/Lucy

Merry Christmas Grandma.

Mo

A very Merry Christmas to you two. Merry Christmas Jane. I thought you were coming in the morning.

Jane

We were, but with his father as he is, he wants to spend as much time as he can with him. Right you two, lets get in. See you later. *(They walk off)*

Janice

It can't be long before she is due?

Mo

They are saying within the next four weeks. Right, we have stood here for over an hour. I'm going in for a warm.

Phoebe

No you are not.

Mo

What do you mean I'm not?

Phoebe

We are going in. But you are waiting out here.

Mo

But it's bloody freezing.

Phoebe

Come on Janice. *(They both walk off)*

Mo is left alone, staring into the darkness. After a couple of minutes, she spots Michael coming up the drive.

Mo

Merry Christmas Michael.

Michael

Merry Christmas Mum. *(They hug for a couple of minutes)* Will you take my arm and I'll lead you in.

Mo

With pleasure.

Mo and Michael are seen walking arm in arm into the manor.

As they walk through the door they can both see Jenny and Lucy dressed in bridesmaid dresses and James and Tommy dressed as page boys. Phoebe and Janice, as the matrons of honour, are holding the children's hands.

Phoebe

Give me your coat, I'll hang it up. *(She does this)*

Mo

Who's getting married?

Michael

You are.

Mo

Don't be silly. Phoebe what's going on?

Phoebe

You see that man at the altar?

Mo

Yes it's Ron.

Phoebe

Well that man loves you so much, he can't live without you any longer.

Janice

They'd better be tears of joy?

Mo

Joy and shock.

Phoebe

Right young lady, wipe your face. *(She gives Mo a handkerchief)* Let's get this wedding started.

The wedding anthem begins. Mo and Michael are seen walking down the aisle with Phoebe and Janice walking behind, holding the children's hands. As Mo and Michael reach the altar, Ron steps forward and gets down on one knee.

Ron
Will you marry me?

Mo
Yes. *(They hold each other. Everyone in the congregation applauds)*

Vicar
Thank goodness for that. *(Everyone laughs)*

As the Vicar goes through the wedding ceremony, Mo notices that Billy is Ron's best man. Billy gives the vicar the rings.

Vicar
I pronounce you man and wife. You may kiss the bride. *(As they kiss, the congregation erupts in a loud applause. Both Ron and Mo are seen walking up the aisle, with the children following. As they reach the door the photographer is at the door to take photos)*

Photographer
Mr & Mrs Johnson, would you like to stand over there so I can have the Manor as the backdrop. *(He takes the picture)* Right can I have the immediate family please *(Michael stands next to his Mother with his hands on Billy's shoulders)* The groom's side please.

Phoebe
Come on Janice, that's us. *(They stand next to Ron)*

Mo
Your Grace, will you stand with us?

The Duke

I'll be very proud to. *(The photographer takes the picture)*

Photographer

Can I have the bridesmaids and the page boys please. *(The camera flashes)* Right is there any more family?

Mo

Yes, all the people you see here today are family. Come on everyone. *(As they all assemble the Duke speaks to Mo)*

The Duke

Now that I have seen you married, I am content with the world. Have a wonderful life together my darling.

Mo

Thank you Your Grace.

Photographer

Smile everyone. *(The picture is taken)*

Michael

Mum we have one more surprise. You see that box at the end of the lawn? I want you both to walk over and press the button. *(As the both walk over, everyone applauds)* Everyone. Three, two, one.

They press the button and the firework display begins. Mo and Ron are seen in each others arms. The snow starts to fall as they kiss

Printed in Poland
by Amazon Fulfillment
Poland Sp. z o.o., Wrocław